The Cairo Sleeper

George Mado has officially left the British Secret Service, but he eagerly exchanges suburban retirement for a flight to the war-torn Middle East on behalf of Greek millionaire Panayotis Marides. His mission: to keep an eye on a delicate situation involving a rich Beiruti banker. It turns out also to involve the KGB, revolution in Cairo, and the notorious defector Paul Tarnham, long believed dead but now masquerading as an Arab sheik.

In Cairo, where the sudden disappearance of Egypt's President has resulted in chaos, Mado joins up with American agent Lars Sweeney and red-headed reporter Andrea Eckersley. Keeping afloat instinctively in the treacherous cross-currents of Middle Eastern affairs, the three colleagues set out to discover who is controlling events. Mustafa Khaliq, the Palestinian terrorist? Henri Bariolet, the banker? His beautiful wife, Micheline? Russia's Colonel Karai? Sammy the Wog, a sinister Cairo club-owner? One of them will be vitally important, will be a catalyst in the coming explosion, will in fact be the Cairo 'sleeper'.

Warren Tute's new thriller is written with his customary inventiveness and expertise, and is an exciting blend of action, sex and political intrigue.

Also by Warren Tute

Novels
The Felthams (1950)
Lady in Thin Armour (1951)
Gentleman in Pink Uniform (1952)
The Younger Felthams (1953)
Girl in the Limelight (1954)
The Cruiser (1955)
The Rock (1957)
Leviathan (1959)
The Golden Greek (1960)
The Admiral (1963)
A Matter of Diplomacy (1969)
The Powder Train (1970)
The Tarnham Connection (1971)
The Resident (1973)
Next Saturday in Milan (1975)
Honours of War and Peace (1976)

History
The Grey Top Hat (1961)
Atlantic Conquest (1962)
Cochrane (1964)
Escape Route Green (1971)
The Deadly Stroke (1973)
Hitler: The Last Ten Days (1973)
D-Day (1974)

Miscellaneous
Chico (1950)
Life of a Circus Bear (1952)
(with Felix Fonteyn) Cockney Cats (1953)
Le Petomane (1967)

Plays
Jessica
A Time to be Born
A Few Days in Greece
Frost at Midnight (translation)
Quartet for Five (translation)

For James Price

with all good wishes

Warren Tute

WARREN TUTE

The Cairo Sleeper

Constable London

First published in Great Britain 1977
by Constable and Company Ltd
10 Orange Street London WC2H 7EG

ISBN 0 09 461330 3

Set in Intertype Plantin

Printed in Great Britain by The Anchor Press Ltd
and bound by Wm Brendon & Son Ltd
both of Tiptree, Essex

I

George Mado lay on his back looking at the ceiling, his right hand nestling comfortably between his wife's ample thighs. It was a bright early summer morning and he decided that on balance he must be enjoying his retirement. Well . . . probably. Just. Anna, his plump Czech wife, had recently given birth to a second daughter, he had no office to go to, no boss to serve, and the Mado semi-detached in Surbiton had sufficient garden to make oapwork an agreeable way of passing an hour or two on a fine day such as this was going to be. Well – and why not? he said to himself.

'Of course I'm rather a tyro at it at present,' he would explain to anyone who asked what oapwork meant, 'strictly speaking, I've only been put out to grass: I'm not legally an old age pensioner for another five years.'

'Senior Citizen is the phrase people are using today,' Anna would remind him with a cautionary frown, 'and I wish you'd keep quiet about your age. Think what it's like for me. From now on I'm telling people you're my father.'

'How about a little early-morning incest, then?' George murmured as he kissed his wife's neck and began gently fondling her gorgeous breasts. Outside the birds chirped away as if their lives depended upon it, and in the next room the new baby began to gurgle and stir about. 'And very jolly it is – this leisured existence, I mean. I can't think why I didn't chuck it all in before. This is the life . . .' he went on, attempting to manoeuvre Anna's well-proportioned body into the right geographical position and receiving a resounding slap on the buttocks for his pains.

'That's enough of that. You crazy or something? I'm just going to feed the baby.'

'Babies can always wait. Your man has a busy day ahead. I'd like to get off to a flying start. Concorde does it in three and a half hours. I think I can improve on that.'

She kissed him and got out of bed.

'You always say you've got a busy day ahead when you've nothing to do at all. What's special about today?'

'Nothing much,' he said, looking at the laburnum tree outside the bedroom window. It was a blaze of yellow like a waterfall of colour. 'I'm lunching with Padstow up in town, and I might have a haircut.'

'You're what?'

Anna stopped dead in her tracks. When she was afraid, her voice became sharp, almost shrill.

'You promised you were through with all that. You've *retired*, George. You've finished with Padstow.'

'Of course. No harm in taking the odd lunch off the firm, though, is there?'

'George!'

'Saves on the housekeeping. I mean, if you work it out on an annual basis . . .'

'George!' she wailed. 'I knew I couldn't trust you. You *promised*. When you retired, you said, you'd never take on another operation again. Never.'

'Who's talking about an operation? It's only a lunch.'

'I know that Padstow and his lunches. I don't trust him an inch. Nor you – you perfidious Albion you . . .' Then came some unintelligible word in Czech.

'Now look here!' Mado said, only too well aware that he'd lost that particular ploy. 'No old age pensioner is going to be talked to in that tone of voice . . . oh! very well, then, Padstow is just an excuse. You see, there was this ravishing blonde with the long mane of hair at the Marideses' the other night – you know, the one with the teeth – well, she wants to get into educational publishing and I thought I'd just . . .'

That didn't work either. She looked so unhappy, he thought he might chuck in his hand. But what could you do about an endless dilemma?

'Merry hell, Anna, when you've been a blown spy as long as I have, you can't just give it up like smoking, can you? I mean, I'm a kind of elder statesman in the game. They actually ask my advice. How about that? I mean, the President of the United States appoints that Robert Murphy as a sort of ombudsman to the CIA and he's over eighty. Now here on this side of the Atlantic, Padstow just simply wants to stand his old mate a dull, dreary lunch at his club . . .'

She stood absolutely still, naked, in the middle of the bedroom, the tears pouring down her cheeks. He got out of bed and put his arms round her.

'Look, darling, it isn't like it used to be,' he said, as if comforting a child. 'I've done my time. I've been through the Lubyanka bit. They're not interested in me for that sort of thing any more. No one's going to abstract me in the middle of the night – not now. The scene has changed. You know that. There are other candidates now for the Gulag archipelago. But if you've spent your whole life in Security, as I have, you can't just drop it all like an old suit because you happen to have sixty on the clock. If Padstow wants to talk something over . . .'

She freed herself, picked up her dressing gown and went through into the children's room.

'In that case,' she said over her shoulder, 'you might just as well have accepted Marides's offer of a retainer for – for what did he call it? – unspecified services.'

'I did,' Mado said, making a wry face at himself in the mirror. 'You don't think I can indulge in all this unpaid oap-work on what the government hands out for a pension, do you? Not after *my* chequered career. By the time those bloody civil servants have finished cutting your entitlement down to size, there's not much more than a cup of coffee in it.'

'Oh God,' Anna said, somehow managing a more cheerful tone of voice, 'why did I marry such a bastard?'

'Because you love me, you old bag, and because I ditto you.'

'Well, whatever he says, you're not to go abroad any more.

'Oh, I wouldn't do a thing like that!' Mado said. 'I couldn't leave Surbiton now. No, it's just a genial chat. That's all he's after. Nothing heavier than that.'

If George Mado had retired from the service, young Mr Padstow – not that he was all that young any more – had decidedly not, and he approached this luncheon with his habitual blend of amusement and misgivings. Would it be wise to involve Mado again? Now that the maverick of M Sixteen (which as a schoolboy he had imagined the department to be called) had really and truly retired, would it not be more expedient to heave a sigh of relief and ask Buggins to take his turn next?

Padstow's immediate chief, that desiccated don of diplomacy, Pryce Yorker, would certainly have adopted the latter course. But then Pryce Yorker in Padstow's opinion was an arrogant tunt, his main pleasure in life, perhaps his only one, being *The Times* crossword puzzle.

Pryce Yorker considered himself a mandarin of Whitehall, but in Padstow's eyes he had a lance-corporal's power of command. Padstow looked on him as a tyrant of the In Tray, whose genuine enthusiasm for the job could be likened to that of an arthritic traffic warden's enthusiasm for her beat on a rainy day. For the umpteenth time Padstow promised himself that if Pryce Yorker stayed much longer *en poste*, if he did nothing about that numbing halitosis he beamed round the building, then he would have no option but to report him to the Secretary of State as an environmental hazard.

But denigrating Pryce Yorker in his thoughts did not get him off the hook with Mado. If Pryce Yorker could be looked on in naval terms as the equivalent of a crusty Admiral Superintendent of a dockyard, Mado was a privateer who, at the drop of a hat, could become a full-scale pirate and an even fuller-scale liability to boot. Mado had graced or disgraced many of Padstow's previous assignments. Mado was at times almost impossible to control. When reminded that his pension might be at risk, Mado had instructed him to stuff his pension right up.

In the end Mado would go his own sweet way, and the trouble was that he often proved to be right. Mado had bought his experience dear. Those cool quizzical eyes could bore holes through any fancy ideas the 'desk wallahs' might be dreaming up. On Padstow's first foreign appointment many years ago, when he had held down the department's desk in Beirut, he had had to deal with Mado on 'Operation Powder Train', and Mado had told him to his face that he was 'upper class thick' – and that was not a scene he relished remembering.

They had crossed swords on many occasions since, but now that Padstow was the boss, now that he was ensconced in his eyrie close to the Cabinet offices, now that he had become the sort of trouble-shooter at the seat of power that Mado had long been in the field, he had acquired an affection for the pug-nosed, whisky-drinking lecher (one of Mado's least damaging descriptions in the records) which Padstow had to admit was based on the simple word 'integrity'.

No intellectual, Mado was 'intelligent' in the French use of the word. He was tough, he was fearless and he was very often funny. But was it a good idea to get him in now on another operation as yet unnamed, not even properly defined, indeed in which British Security had little more than a watching brief? On the spur of the moment he decided it was not. He would put it off. He picked up the phone and rang Mado at home. Anna answered.

'Is he there?' Padstow asked. 'We're supposed to be meeting for lunch and . . .'

'I'm afraid he's already left. Is there any message I can take?'

'No, no. I'll tell him myself when I see him at the club.'

'Mr Padstow,' Anna said with a break in the voice. 'He's supposed to have retired. Don't you people ever think of the wives?'

Padstow hesitated a moment before replying. He was slightly taken aback.

'Well yes, Mrs Mado, we do. We think a lot of the wives. But this is purely a social engagement.'

'Like hell and high water,' Anna said in her heavy Czech accent and put down the phone. As usual she had got the metaphor muddled.

Down in Sunningdale, Panayotis Marides, the Greek multimillionaire, 'the only Greek proud of a British passport', strode up and down the library, as he was pleased to call it, of the vast mock-Tudor mansion he had bought in order that his newborn son could grow up against the proper background of an English gentleman.

'I don't know what you're so angry about,' his wife Elissa remarked. In fact she knew perfectly well what had set him going, but she was not letting herself be cheated of a feminine pleasure in compelling him to put it into words.

'Those-a Fleet Street hags!' Marides snorted. 'God save us from the British press!'

'But Andrea Eckersley's an old friend – and a very attractive woman. I suppose what actually happened was that you made a pass at her and got your usual rebuff.'

'You know what she hadda the nerve to say? To me – Panayotis Marides?'

He attempted to imitate the way Andrea held herself, failing in this completely and looking to Elissa's eyes like an elderly drag artiste unsure of his material.

'She's one of the top feature writers in the country,' Elissa said.

'Yach!' said Marides, pouring himself a large ouzo from the decanter on his desk and slumping into his great chair with the high carved back. 'Justa because she has red hair, nice tits and her father's an earl, she thinks she has the right to patronise a poor Greek from a mountain village?'

When Marides was angry, he would often adopt a fake Greek-American accent and then equally suddenly revert to his normal and nearly perfect control of the English tongue. Elissa thought he did it out of boredom.

'Good heavens! What on earth did she say that's got you going like this?'

'She asks why I call my son Winston.'

'Well, what's so terrible about a question like that?'

'I said, "You want I should call him Mao or Vladimir Trotsbottom or some other stinking Communist name? I call him Winston because thatsa the name of the greatest Englishman this century has seen." And then do you know what she said?'

'Surprise me.'

'She put that smirk on her face and asked "Is it a barony you're after, Pan, or would you be satisfied with a mere knighthood?"'

Elissa laughed and kissed him on the top of his head as he sat, a compressed mound of energy, like an off-duty Cardinal.

'Well, it *is* what you're after, isn't it? You've got almost everything else. By the way, Pan, have you really put George Mado on retainer?'

She knew he hated being asked questions of that sort and

now he shot her a hard, penetrating look, as if she herself were asking for a job.

'So what?'

'It's only that the Mados have a new baby, too – as well you know.'

'A girl,' Marides said, as if that put a stop to it all.

'Are you going to expose that poor man to danger in the way you have done before?'

Marides gave another of his famous snorts.

'You his agent or something? Whatsa you trying to say? Mado has never worked for me before. Always he is a British Government man. What are you on about now?'

'Whether or not you've actually paid him money before, you know as well as I do that George Mado has been deeply involved with you in four or five big operations . . .'

She lit a cigarette and walked over to the window which looked down on the formal garden, a miniature caricature of Blenheim which she privately thought to be in terrible taste but which, she was delighted to recognise, gave her exceptional husband an enormous and childish pleasure to own.

'You know what happened on the last two occasions,' she went on after a pause; 'your enemies – or, if you don't want to call them that, the "hostile element" – abducted me and they also took in Anna, George's wife. I don't know what you're up to this time, Pan, but they may perfectly well try it again.'

'You think the security of this house needs attention? I tell you I have every conceivable electronic device wired into every conceivable security force . . .'

'Yes, Pan, I'm aware of all that. The Berlin Bunker has nothing on this modest dwelling. However, if you *are* going to involve George Mado in more danger abroad, then I'd like to ask Anna and her children to move into the second chauffeur's cottage while the heat is on. We owe them a little care and attention.'

'Ask anyone you like,' Pan said, 'but you're wasting your time. I have no operation on hand.'

'Then what was Lars Sweeney doing here yesterday afternoon? Lars is never around just for social reasons.'

'He's never around when you're here alone,' Marides cut in with one of his sudden smiles, 'I tell you I see to that!'

Lars Sweeney, Marides's American lawyer, had been instrumental in fixing up their marriage after what came to be called the Tarnham Connection had been dissolved. Elissa had previously been married to Paul Tarnham, late of the Foreign Office and England's most celebrated defector since Philby. Marides was grateful for Sweeney's 'instrumentality' but he remained what he had been born – a Greek peasant with all the suspicious sense of possession that a Greek countryman has for his wife and family.

Although Marides had become one of the world's richest men, he had in no way abandoned the standards he would have maintained in the Pindus mountain village from which he had sprung. Lars Sweeney was a cultured Bostonian, a spare and attractive man. Marides did not lose sleep about any man Elissa had happened to fancy before he married her: now that she was his wife, however, the door to her bedroom was to be kept firmly locked when Caesar was away.

In this he completely misjudged Elissa, who now had no sexual interest in any man other than himself. But she did not take offence at the precautions his nature forced him to require. Had he been any different, he would not have been the Panayotis Marides to whom she had given her life – or what was left of it after the wreckage Tarnham had caused.

'Well, Pan,' she said, 'I never ask questions you're unlikely to answer.'

'So don't,' he growled.

'But you brought us to England so that your son could be born an Englishman . . .'

'Yes, yes, yes. I know what you're trying to find out.' He paused for a moment or so, and then went on gruffly, 'I'll put it this way. I go to Teheran and Peking next week, as you know, and you're joining me in California when that trip is over. In the meantime I'm sending Sweeney and Mado out to Beirut. I don't trust that Bariolet and his Libyan–Iraqui connections.'

'Beirut! That's a healthy city these days.'

This was the summer of 1976 and the civil war had already begun.

'So Mado and Sweeney can keep an eye on certain of my interests there,' Marides said, lighting a cigar. 'That Bariolet and his bank . . .'

'Doesn't that Bariolet have a very attractive wife?'

'He has a sexy English wife, a palace in Beirut, a summer house in Alexandria, a town house in Cairo, a yacht nearly as big as my own – what else you want I should tell you? I just don't like some of his friends.'

'I think I'll give Anna Mado a call this afternoon. She's going to be pretty unhappy about what you've just said.'

'When you are on the payroll,' Marides said with a granite look in the eyes, 'you do as you're told.'

It was unlike Mado to be late, especially when there was a prospect of freeloading in a gentleman's club. Padstow wriggled in irritation in the basement bar of the Pall Mall establishment, looking out at the sombre garden into which nobody seemed to go. Around him ambassadors and their ilk mingled with other taipans of the higher civil service, standing each other the ritual sherry before going upstairs to the big front room for luncheon.

As most members of the club worked in Whitehall the bar was packed between 12.45 and 1.15 p.m., and then, like a flock of migrating swallows, off they would swoop as they did now, leaving Padstow puzzled and slightly uneasy. It was not a good omen.

He wished yet again that he had never thought of involving Mado at all. Moreover, he resented being crabbed and confined – in the usual way of the service – by not being able to brief Mado except in the vaguest terms. Never let the man in the field know more than the essential minimum. That way you lessen the risk all round.

But when that man happened to be Mado, you had a rough passage selling the deal at all, and today Padstow himself had only the vaguest idea of what Mado or anyone else would be likely to find when they actually got to work. As on the last occasion in Rome, when there was supposed to be some devilish event about to happen 'next Saturday in Milan', so this time all that Padstow could reveal about the situation was that something was moving in the Middle East, something at present undefined, something big and apparently without limits – or any other features by which to set it in context.

Padstow ordered another Campari and soda and cursed Mado for being late. This needlessly increased his nervous strain – the last thing he wanted. He had to grant one quality to Pryce Yorker, his grotty boss: Pryce Yorker seemed devoid of any emotional tension at all. He appeared able to deal with the big and small crises of daily departmental life as if he were some bloodless professor looking out on the quadrangle of a minor college, impervious to the problems of lesser mortals, living a dried-out life according to a scale of human values which Padstow, who liked human beings, could only dub intolerable. But perhaps just such a small intellectual ticker was what was wanted at the top. Drat the man, Padstow said to himself, using a phrase which had been a favourite of his grandfather's, drat the man Mado – why was he late?

By two o'clock when Mado had still not arrived, nor had he phoned, Padstow decided to go upstairs for a plate of cold meat and afterwards to return to the Cabinet offices. Then, on his way through the hall, he observed Mado striding into the club, an unaccustomed scowl on his face. He was moving in what Padstow's grandfather would have described as a 'thorough-going fluster'.

'I asked you to lunch, not dinner.'

'Turn around, sport. Lead me down to the bar. I need a stiff drink.'

'I've never known you want anything else.'

He bought the pug-faced man a double Scotch and then they moved to a far corner of the almost deserted bar.

'So who is she this time?' Padstow asked. 'Blonde? Brunette? I sincerely hope above the age of consent?'

'Fasten your seat belt, friend, you're in for a bumpy ride. I've just seen Tarnham.'

Padstow stared at him with an amused smile.

'You'll have to dry out, George. The next step is going to be DTs and you won't like that at all.'

'I tell you I've just seen . . .'

'Tarnham was killed in an ambush in Czechoslovakia eight years ago. You know that as well as I do. I suppose you've just seen him walking hand in hand with Jean-Pierre Mournier?' Padstow went on with heavy sarcasm, 'I suppose you saw Mournier too. You may remember Tarnham and Mournier cancelled each other out.'

'Those eyes I never forget,' Mado said, looking into the distance and taking a long pull at his drink.

'Oh, come on, George, get a grip on yourself!'

'Listen, sport, I'm sitting in a bus in Piccadilly, aren't I – as you didn't send me an official conveyance – and alongside comes an embassy car with two Arabs in the back seat. They were decked out in the full outfit – white burnouse, kufia, the lot. One of them was Tarnham. We all stopped at the lights. I leapt out, commandeered the first car I could find and gave chase.'

'You *what*? In Piccadilly?'

'The car I picked on happened to be driven by an American tourist.'

Mado tried, and failed, to suppress a grin.

'I think he was showing his wife some of the sights. Well, I certainly made *their* day! They took a little persuading and by that time the embassy car was almost out of sight. However, with Mado at the wheel we crashed the lights – zoom – zap! and I drove like Boanerges towards Knightsbridge.'

'Like who?'

'Never mind. I drove at reprehensible speed.'

'Did you catch them up?'

'No,' Mado said, pursing his lips, 'I did not. I got stuck behind one of those bloody Common Market lorries that are supposed to be banned from the West End. By the time I'd got around that, they'd disappeared towards Queen's Gate – at least I think that's where they went. Anyway, I lost them.'

'And then you had a little explaining to do?'

'The Americans had some bizarre notion of calling the police . . .'

'But you soon put a stop to that?'

'I gave them the Mado charm and that was no small feat in the circumstances, I can tell you. The wife put it down to driving on the left. Anyway we parted good friends. As a matter of fact, they've asked me to come and stay in South Dakota. It's Sioux country. Me Big Buffalo Chief Mado . . .'

He paused and gave Padstow a grinding look.

'Well, sport, so what do you make of that? Do you believe me? Or do I take a one-way trip to the funny farm?'

Padstow sat very quiet and still. For a while neither of them said a word. Padstow looked steadily at Mado whose eyes flickered from his glass to Padstow and back again.

At last Padstow said in a very small voice, 'I'm afraid I have to believe you, George. The – the renaissance of Tarnham was something you of all people could not be told. But now you've found out . . .'

Mado took a deep breath and then let it out.

'You bastard!' he said. 'The only man in Whitehall I trusted.'

'Trust, George. You can still trust. Nothing has changed. You know the rules.'

'Sod the rules! If Tarnham was never killed . . . if he's had the nerve to come back here to this country, masquerading as an Arab. . . .' He faltered into silence, overcome by the enormity of the idea. 'The most celebrated defector there's even been . . .'

'Let's see if there's some food left upstairs,' Padstow said, carefully watching his guest. 'This wasn't a part of the plan, but I'll now put you in the picture just as much as I possibly can.'

As soon as she had finished the Marides interview, the Lady Andrea Eckersley – who kept the 'Lady' part as far in the background as possible – returned to Fulham, where she shared a small house in a quiet road with her photographer brother.

She knew Panayotis had ruffled up at her crack about the peerage, but she felt that any wound she had inflicted would be regarded as superficial. Underneath she considered that Pan liked her. At the very least she knew he found her attractive. Each appreciated where the other stood on any matter of importance. Both had understanding – at least of a kind. Both looked on life as something of a game, given the rules might differ for each.

This was not the first piece she had written about the international multi-millionaire. Doubtless it would not be the last. In spite of the great man's decision to pull out of the Middle East and concentrate on Iran and China, the Marides empire would inevitably continue to exercise power in the area where his extraordinary career had begun. Oil was still oil and shipping, shipping.

En route, as she would soon be, to Cairo and to other Arab capitals for her 'Profile Portfolio' of the current men at the top, she would still make use of the guidelines of power, or at any rate of the many invaluable facilities which the Marides Organisation could put at her disposal once the boss had indicated that she was *persona grata*. As, in fact, she was.

Her brother was just leaving on his Yamaha for some photographic assignment. Spencer had opted for photography as an agreeable way of getting through the early part of his life. 'Taking snaps' had not been their father's idea of a suitable profession for someone who would one day be the fourteenth Earl, but then equally their father had found it a bit batty that his only daughter, having made it to Oxford against intense competition, should now mess about in Fleet Street, as he put it, digging up dirt for some dreary gossip column or other. His two children had long defeated the thirteenth Earl, who preferred to concentrate what attention he could muster, after alcohol had taken its toll, on his Dorset estate, and also on becoming as little involved as possible in his wife's social activities.

'That American rang up again,' Spencer said, as he started the machine and prepared to set off, looking like a hominoid from outer space. 'Wants you to go to some wog embassy with him tonight.'

'Lars Sweeney?'

'That's the man. He's at the Connaught. Would you ring him back?'

She turned this over quietly in her mind as she went up to her workroom. What did Lars Sweeney want? She knew one obvious answer to that – herself, in bed. And that was not such a revolting idea. Lars was a good-looking, jokey character who would grace anybody's swimming pool, and who could even survive a weekend in an English country house such as her parents' and be asked again.

She knew that Marides had used him as an oil lawyer for a number of years, and that Sweeney also had some sort of connection with the CIA. But then, who didn't these days? She had been slightly caught up with him and with George Mado in Greece at the time the Russian KGB Resident Voznitsky had made his spectacular dash for the West. She had been similarly involved in Rome when Mustafa Khaliq and the Pan Islamic Terrorist Organisation had made life unbearably hot.

She was quite fond of Lars Sweeney, but decided she liked him better at arm's length. Wryly she confessed to herself that this was a decision she seemed to come to about most of the men she met in the course of her working life. Perhaps that's why she was so often thought to be gay, she said to herself as she called the Connaught and asked for Mr Sweeney. But then, did you ever really know about anyone else's inner life? It was a tricky enough business getting to know yourself in the time at your disposal these days.

The Arab Embassy to which she and Lars Sweeney duly repaired for an early-evening reception could be counted among the most spacious (and specious, as her brother would have added) in that deserted area of South Kensington now given over to the Corps Diplomatique. Money was literally no object. Indeed, the embassy in question held the record for parking fines acquired by its staff during the course of any one day, for the lavishness of its hospitality – they were alleged to shred up fivers and serve them with the caviare – for an almost total bureaucratic incompetence and for the charm of its ambassador and his entourage, especially where women were concerned. In the corridors of London diplomacy, this embassy was known simply as Mecca.

On this particular evening it would not have been an

exaggeration to say that the London equivalent of *tout Paris* was milling about the main salon. The pound that day had fallen to a new low, and everyone was holding a glass of champagne.

Panayotis and Elissa were there, as were the other half-dozen Greek and Levantine tycoons and their wives who made the running in oil and shipping in the Middle East. Padstow was there, with two of the more senior Deputy Under-Secretaries of State at the Foreign Office. Also present were such public figures as the Head of the Confederation of British Industries, the current *éminence grise* of the Trades Union Congress, the Foreign Editor of *The Times*, a senior director from each of the eight main oil companies of the world, and what seemed to be a small army of sheiks from every desert in Arabia and of Arab city men in western clothing.

'I'm glad you called me,' Andrea said to Lars Sweeney as they went into the embassy, 'I hate facing this mob on my own.'

'I thought you women libbers were adept at keeping the boys at bay.'

'You mean the hard ice underneath is showing through?'

'Did the Prophet himself not remark that no ice endureth for long in the desert sun?'

She and Lars usually fenced in this way when they had not been together for some time. Andrea pretended to carry it off with an air, but in fact was privately dismayed by the impression she seemed to give of frigidity. She consoled herself by remembering that at times it could be a useful shield.

'This ice maiden can and does endure,' she said, as an especially lascivious Lebanese politician she had known in Rome espied her and set off towards her through the throng, a smirk of anticipation on his face.

'You're no ice maiden to me,' Lars said, and meant it.

'You've made a date for dinner with me when this phantasmagoria is over. Don't forget.'

'Big words get you nowhere – particularly big words I couldn't spell.'

The Beiruti was almost upon them. From then on there would be little chance of any private talk.

'Is there anyone here you feel you have to contact?'

She looked puzzled, so Lars went on quickly, 'I mean, you have your profile itinerary for the Middle East fully mapped out?'

'Oh! I see. Yes, more or less. It's mostly Kings and Presidents.'

She could never be sure of the extent to which Lars Sweeney had been briefed about her background activities. Generally speaking, the press and intelligence kept themselves wisely apart. Each could be bad news for the other. Both could so easily contaminate not only themselves but their support systems – and indeed any project with which they were known to be concerned.

For instance, although she and Padstow, whom she now spotted across the room talking to an Egyptian General, had more than an understanding between them, both pretended to be strangers whenever they accidentally met at parties such as this. In fact, only her brother knew how close a connection she had with young Mr Padstow and the little ex-housemaid's room in Downing Street which he used as an office.

'It is excellent you are coming to visit war-torn Beirut.' The squat Lebanese bowed unzipping her with a searing look. 'For a proper understanding of the situation in Beirut, Damascus and Cairo, I think there is someone here you should meet. He goes back there tomorrow and he is known to Monsieur Henri Bariolet, the eminent banker. Pray follow me, Miss Eckersley. I told the Sheik I would bring you across.'

Lars Sweeney nodded her a temporary farewell with a smile.

'That last question of mine looks kind of superfluous,' he said, 'but don't forget you're bespoke for dinner tonight.'

'Such a charming American,' the Beiruti politician murmured, studying her with a sideways look as they threaded their way across the party. 'Mr Sweeney, I mean. But we are always a little sad when our friends spend too much time with the CIA.' Then, before Andrea could comment on this, he went on, 'I had a meeting with Mustafa Khaliq a few days ago and he mentioned your name . . .' They were approaching a tall, distinguished-looking man in a white burnouse. This was evidently the Sheik. 'Mustafa Khaliq said you must be sure to get in touch with him when you are out in our part of the world. You and the Leader were at Oxford together, were you not?'

'And more recently in Rome,' Andrea said drily. 'How are things these days with PITO?'

'Ah! that side of things I do not know. You will have to ask him about the Pan-Islamic Treaty Organisation yourself when you meet him.'

'Treaty? I thought the T stood for Terrorist.'

The Beiruti laughed in an insincere, mirthless way. The mouth smiled but the eyes were cold.

'I think there are several matters on which your Ladyship is a little out of date. No doubt Sheik Karim al Hammad will help you to understand how things really are in the Middle East.'

The Sheik bowed gravely and addressed her in faultless English. The burnouse effectively framed and disguised his real appearance, but there was something familiar about the dark fanatic eyes which Andrea could not immediately place. Perhaps this was just as well, since, had she known then the true identity of this man who seemed oddly concerned that she should visit him in Damascus rather than casually exchanging small talk at an embassy party, she might have been nonplussed as to what to do. Certainly it was lucky that

George Mado had not been asked. There would then have been no need for him to leap off a bus in Piccadilly and commandeer a car.

'You are a friend of the Marideses, are you not?' the Sheik was saying. She could see Pan and Elissa in a far corner, and she remembered afterwards that the Sheik seemed to take especial care to keep his back turned on them and would move a hand up to his face if any risk occurred of his being observed in a nearby mirror.

'I hear Kyria Marides has just presented him with a son.' As he said this a cynical smile seemed to play around his sensual mouth, another fact she remembered when thinking over the meeting afterwards.

'I also hear that our Chinese friends are taking up more and more of Marides's time these days. So perhaps it is fortunate that Henri and Micheline Bariolet – with whom, perhaps, you may be staying in Cairo and Beirut, if their house survives – remain firmly wedded to the Middle Eastern scene. I suppose Bariolet must be the only serious rival Marides faces these days in the eastern Mediterranean.'

'Your Highness is very well-informed,' Andrea said. 'If you should ever want a job in Fleet Street . . .'

'I'll know where to come,' he said drily, with a kind of tortured smile. 'Unfortunately I cannot be here for long. I would love to have spent a few days at Lord's. The game means so much to me and I see it so rarely. Incidentally, talking of cricket,' he went on, before she could interrupt, 'what is your presidential batting order for the profiles you are writing? Are you putting in Syria before Egypt? Iraq before Libya?'

'I haven't decided,' Andrea said, watching him intently. 'Why? Does it matter?'

'Of course not, and it is none of my business. The British press has always been a law unto itself. But I am still interested to know whom you are seeing and when. You must understand that most of them are my friends. Or at any rate friends of friends, if you know what I mean.'

'I'm not sure that I do.'

'Then we shall have to enlighten you, won't we?' the Sheik said, rather in the manner of a general giving orders to his ADC. With a polite nod he indicated that the audience was over and began moving away.

'Now let me procure you another glass of champagne,' the Beiruti politician said, seizing her hand in a clammy grip and leading her away. She caught sight of Lars's raised eyebrows across the room and made a face at him. The CIA was going to have to wait. But what did the Sheik imply by 'friend of a friend'? And how would she be enlightened?

2

'So we must be careful,' Sheik Karim al Hammad declared a few days later to a meeting of 'friends' and 'friends of friends' at the Soviet Embassy in Beirut. 'Her Press Ladyship has a sharp and enquiring mind. I noticed that she seemed to be surprised at the amount we knew of her movements – or her proposed movements out here. Surprise leads almost at once to suspicion; suspicion to enquiry and enquiry to the discovery of matters which are none of her business, or rather which *should* be none of her business.'

'I could have told you that,' said Mustafa Khaliq. He neither liked nor respected this pseudo-Sheik who would appear and then vanish without warning, and to whom even General Simonov and Colonel Karai of the KGB had to defer in a way which those two arrogant men must have found highly distasteful. 'I had to deal with her in Rome. Why is it necessary to tell her anything at all?'

'The PITO leader should ask questions which concern his organisation and nothing else,' Karim said sharply, with a glance at Simonov and Karai. 'Mustafa Khaliq will no doubt remember that *we* had to deal with *him* in Rome, if that is the phrase he wishes to use.'

Khaliq reacted to this with a sullen glare. He was not enjoying himself. The Pan-Islamic Terrorist Organisation depended essentially on the Russians for money, arms and supplies. The Russians were hard taskmasters, however, and they exacted a high price for their support. At times it seemed to Khaliq that they regarded his organisation as no better than some dockside gang, a bunch of intimidators assignable to any particularly dirty job, from abduction to murder, which the KGB did not wish to undertake itself.

'We are neither thugs nor gangsters,' he had become tired of explaining. 'We are freedom fighters for Palestine. We have the right to be heard.'

This did not go down well with the KGB. 'Keep that sort of bourgeois-capitalist statement for the bourgeois-capitalists who may or may not be interested,' they curtly informed him. The Russian outlook remained simple: 'You want our guns, you want our money, so you obey orders. And we give the orders.'

'Very well,' Khaliq said, narrowing his eyes, 'the PITO leader will confine himself, as you say, to what concerns the organisation. So what is the Egyptian affair to do with PITO? And why should we have to be careful about a visiting English journalist? What is Andrea Eckersley to do with us or with the Egyptian plan?'

A silence fell on the basement room in which the conference was taking place. General Simonov of the KGB glanced at his hatchet man, Colonel Karai, with wordless disapproval. Karim al Hammad reassumed inside himself the upper-class English identity of Paul Tarnham into which he had been born and stared with a nasty disdain at the PITO leader. Altogether there was a black cloud of plain hatred floating about the room. Nevertheless, this Oxford-trained Arab guerrilla would have to be properly answered. PITO was an essential muscle in the body of this operation.

'Ideologically,' Tarnham said, 'the Egyptian affair has nothing to do with PITO.'

'So?' Khaliq demanded.

'PITO is merely a part of the executive end of the plan. I do not have to answer the questions which seem to be worrying the PITO leader. I merely observe that the presence of this British woman journalist may – I only say may – affect the timing. She may enter the line of fire at an awkward time, in which case she will have to be removed. On the other hand, she may conceivably be of use. She is known to have Marxist sympathies.'

'How?' Khaliq went on with relentless obstinacy. 'How can an outsider such as Andrea Eckersley be of use? Or is she a part of the plan about which PITO is not to be informed?'

'You ask too many questions,' General Simonov cut in, lighting a long Russian cigarette and throwing him a caustic look. 'You were told in Rome. I tell you again. We do the briefing. You carry out the orders. Is that understood? Perhaps the Sheik will continue as if no interruption had taken place.'

'Sheik . . .' Khaliq muttered, and then added in Arabic a short phrase roughly translated as 'Sheik my arse.' It was not a happy time for Palestinians.

If there had been a strained atmosphere in the Russian Embassy cellar, it was nothing to the pall of despair which enveloped Beirut and the whole of the Lebanon during the summer of 1976. The civil war had dragged on for over a year, and the Beirut of smart hotels, prosperity and a sophisticated life had by now disappeared almost without a trace.

The wrecked city had become very different from the Beirut George Mado had known in the days of Operation Powder Train. It would have stretched his imagination to breaking point now to call Lebanon the Switzerland of the Middle East. Important firms were moving or had already moved their headquarters to Athens or Cairo. Beirut was not exactly the place for a holiday by the sea.

Indeed, what with the Syrians on one side and the Israelis on the other, the luckless majority of Lebanese who only wanted to get back to doing business and to hell with religion and politics perforce had to continue their daily lives under the crushing intimidation of the Palestinian Left, which in turn took its orders from Moscow.

'Of course that nice Mr Brush Off and Mr Cosy Gin put their jolly smiling faces behind *détente*,' Mado said, as he sat in an office of what was left of the Marides International building in Ras-Beirut. 'Look what it's done for them here in Beirut. They'll soon have this place as Day Tonted as Ulster.'

He looked across the desk at Lars Sweeney who had just walked in after a courtesy visit to the American Embassy.

'So when do we get to meet the Sheik?' he went on, and then as Lars was about to speak, decided to answer his own question. 'I'll tell you what you found out at the embassy. No one has heard of Sheik Karim al Hammad. The guy does not exist. So, of course, who's going to set up a meeting with a myth?'

'That was more or less the message.'

'What about the great banker – Henri Bariolet?'

'He, too, seems to be elusive. No one could tell me whether he's in Beirut or not. This whole place is dying on its feet. They did say that Bariolet is the last of the big ones to move his headquarters to Cairo. I guess that's where the action is – with Micheline minding the summer palace at Alexandria.'

'I dare say,' Mado said thoughtfully, 'but our KGB friends remain here in Beirut. Simonov, Karai and Company Unlimited. They're not moving to Egypt. They need to be here to keep stirring the pot.'

'They can't go back. At least they can't operate in Egypt like they can here. They were thrown out. Sure, they'd be glad to get a grip on Egypt again if they could, but the Sadat-men don't have a treaty of friendship with the Russians any more. They know what a "friendship" treaty means. They've had one good dose of infestation. They're in no hurry to try it again.'

Mado pursed his mouth and looked out on the smashed streets of Beirut.

'So what's it all about? I mean, as far as you and I are concerned? There's a lot doesn't add up,' he went on, 'not that I was ever the top boy at sums. However, Lars, what are you and I really doing here?'

'Living it up at Pan's expense,' Sweeney replied with a smile, 'that is, if you care to call *this* eating high on the hog.' He gestured at the wreckage outside as an armoured car rumbled by.

'That's what I mean – why did Pan send us here? You, I can understand. You're his lawyer. But what am I supposed to be doing? The Bariolet interest seems a bit nebulous to me.'

'Well, you know Pan – he never shows his hand early in the game. I suppose your focal point is Tarnham, or rather Sheik Karim al Hammad.'

'But Pan doesn't know about that.'

'Want to lay a bet?'

'In any case it's nothing to do with Pan.' There was a grim expression in Mado's eyes. 'Tarnham or the Sheik – that's a little private matter for me.'

Lars was watching his old colleague and friend with a mixture of amusement and despair.

'Revenge, George?' He shook his head. 'Okay, so revenge is sweet, Byron said, but he implied it was only women who concerned themselves with revenge. It's not your scene. Revenge is an out-of-date emotion.'

'Well, it's still in date with me,' Mado said grittily. 'I grant you whatever pressure it stokes up in me is cool to icy these days – however, it's very much there. Look, my friend,' he went on with a very hard glint in the eye, 'when you tot up what that man has on his – I was going to say conscience only *that* he doesn't possess – let's say on whatever part of his anatomy where a tally is kept, then revenge is merely another word for the settlement of some ancient debts.'

Sweeney was not disposed to argue about this, so for a moment there was a silence between them. Eventually he said, 'I wonder how long our people and yours have known – I mean that your great British defector was still a part of the scene?'

'You don't supposes Jean-Pierre Mournier is also alive? That whole shooting affray in Czechoslovakia in 1968 a put-up job?'

Sweeney shook his head.

'Mournier's different. That guy was never of particular use to the Russians. No, I guess Mournier's well and truly in the ground. But your Paul Tarnham was an Arabist, a breed very much in demand. A highly expert man. He'd long known his way around the Middle East. The Kremlin would consider him far too valuable to lose in that way.'

'So what's he really doing now?' Mado looked at his nails and decided they needed a manicure. This led to his thinking that a little feminine massage would tone him up generally. But where was he going to get that in war-torn Beirut? He returned to the problem of Tarnham. 'It can't be just the local scene here in Lebanon – Simonov and Karai can take care of that. And what brought Tarnham to London? Even decked out in his fancy Arab outfit, the danger must have been considerable. There's no statute of limitation on treason. At least not as far as I know. He could still have taken a one-way trip to the Tower.'

'No doubt it was a calculated risk. No doubt he had protection. You British seem to have Marxists in the marrow these days: they used to be under the bed.'

'Yes,' Mado agreed thoughtfully, 'a little Whitehall protection, that's the likeliest guess the way things are these days. Our great and gorgeous civil service seems to be poisoned by a sort of creeping collectivism – the only real loyalty being to a continuing socialist creed whatever government happens to be in power. It's the Establishment sleepers we're after – or rather I'm after. God knows there are plenty of those weevilling away.'

'As you're out here in the Middle East, you should look for them here in Beirut or in Cairo first,' Lars said, and then added with a smile, 'I never realised what a political man you are.'

'I never was until that bastard Philby and his running mate Tarnham defected. That's when I had to think for myself.'

'Well, it doesn't seem to have done you much harm,' Sweeney concluded. 'Now let's bend our minds to getting to the great Beiruti banker, Monsieur Henri Bariolet.'

'Protection! Protection!' Micheline Bariolet snapped angrily at her husband as they surveyed the damage to their house in Ras-Beirut. 'What sort of protection is this? I never understand why you continue to play these silly games. *C'est idiot*.'

Both were bilingual in French and English but when alone usually spoke in French.

'What silly games?'

'Imagining you can keep in with both sides. Paying them both. *C'est fou.* They simply take your money and laugh in your face. *Moi – j'en ai marre. Ah! non! ça c'est trop. C'est pas une plaisanterie.* You can do what you like with your PITOs and your Phalangists. I've had enough. I'm going back to Cairo.'

'I ask myself why you pretend to the French,' Henri Bariolet remarked tersely, 'because when you are angry you become *tout à fait anglaise*.'

'If you're going to be clever, get it right. I'm not English, I'm Welsh.'

Bariolet shrugged his shoulders.

'*Si tu veux*. You know how I hate these rows.'

'I dare say you do. I hate having my house destroyed and then looted.'

'That's not exactly my fault.'

She glared at him and tossed her head angrily. He had once

called her 'a lioness when aroused'. 'And you're a monkey,' she had retorted, 'clever, clever, clever. . . .' She had been on the point of driving this home with a sexual parallel but had stopped short at hurting him in that way. He was hopeless in bed and both of them knew it, but because basically she had once been fond of this elderly French-Lebanese whom she had married as her fourth husband, she took care not to go too far. Nevertheless, she would provoke a good shouting match when it suited her simply to keep him under control and get her way.

'I'm not sure it isn't your fault,' she said, picking up the pieces of a valuable Chinese vase which lay beside an overturned table. 'I don't know what you get up to in that dreary bank of yours. You're supposed to make money, not hand it out to terrorists, Russians, Christians and the good God knows who else. I should have married Marides. He's not a fool in that way.'

'Be reasonable, Micheline. I assure you I've done everything I could.'

'Well, *you* can stay here in this pigsty if that's what you want. *Moi, je m'en fous.* I'm going back to Cairo. There is no point whatever in my being here. I don't know why you asked me to come. I suppose the idea was to get me killed in the next riot – so then you'd be free. Where's Suleiman? Where's Hassan?'

Bariolet looked at her wearily. 'Where is anyone these days?'

'Well, what am I to do? Clean the place up myself? Be my own servant? *Ah! non, non, no.* It's too much . . .'

She suddenly caught sight of two strangers picking their way across the rubble of the hall.

'Monsieur?' she called out in a peremptory tone of authority.

'*Bon jour, Madame,*' Mado said jauntily. '*Je cherche Monsieur et Madame Bariolet.*'

She nodded her head in an unwelcoming way. Bariolet simply stared at Mado and at his companion, a hook-nosed Lebanese club owner by the name of Ulf Achmed Aziz.

'I am Sheik Karim al Hammad,' Mado said, 'and this is General Simonov of the KGB or you can call him Colonel Karai, if you like. Well, you can call him anything you like. Aziz won't mind. Will you, Ulf Achmed?'

Micheline's mood was transformed in a flash.

'How very engaging!' she said, shaking his hand. 'You must be George Mado. I heard you were coming to Beirut.'

'*Moi, je ne trouve pas ça amusant,*' Bariolet said curtly.

'I didn't think you would,' Mado replied easily, 'but there seems to be no normal way of arranging a meeting. No messages get through.'

'Who sent you? The British Intelligence?'

'Oh! come on, sport, they're not quite as stupid as that. In any case I've given it up – like wanking. No, I'm working these days for Panayotis Marides.'

'You are wasting your time, Monsieur Mado. When Marides and I have anything to say to each other we say it direct.'

'*Mon dieu!* don't be so stuffy, Henri,' Micheline said. She and Mado had already exchanged a mutually appraising look. That deep-seated, lively and instant question-and-answer had flashed in their eyes. For the first time that day she smiled. She no longer felt bored by the catastrophe to their house and all the trouble in that direction which lay ahead.

'And who is this gentleman?' she asked, nodding at Ulf Achmed Aziz.

'Mr Aziz is a very old friend of mine from the days when Beirut was Beirut. He runs students' clubs and that sort of thing. Very useful if you happen to run out of grass. He can also process grass in another way, if you know what I mean. He is a friend of your son.'

This had an effect on Micheline as if she had been crossing a field on a country walk and had suddenly become aware of a bull snorting in a far corner and looking her way.

'Ah, yes,' she said carefully, 'Pemberton.'

She studied Mr Aziz, whose dark hooded eyes gave nothing away. Bariolet made a gesture of impatience.

'I must get back to the bank,' he said to Micheline. 'Sayyid can drop me off and then take you back to the Clareville.'

The Clareville was one of the smaller hotels in a safer part of the Avenue de Paris, which still functioned because the enterprising management had early on installed its own generator. It was also in an area of the city of no tactical importance to the Palestinian guerrillas, so it had not been touched. Bariolet stumped off to the front door of the mansion, and after a moment's hesitation Micheline followed with Mado and Aziz just behind.

'Where can I find you?' she said to Mado as they made their way through the wrecked hall.

'Dickinson at the embassy or Theodakis at Marides International will usually know where I am. But don't call me, I'll call you,' he added with a twinkle which Micheline returned.

For all the light banter, Mado felt uncomfortably aware of the tension and danger into which he had plunged. Superimposed on the distant rumble of gunfire came the much nearer, intermittent and irregular burst of machine-gun spatting, the abruptness of which – and the short silence with which they were followed – adding to the eerie sensation of danger swirling invisibly yet almost palpably about the ruined mansion. This is no place for a decent British oapman, Mado told himself as he reached the door. The sooner he could scarper out of it the better.

Bariolet had gone ahead and Mado was just moving to one side to let Madame Bariolet follow when there was a sharp clatter of machine-gun fire outside the great door, followed by some confused shouting in Arabic. Grabbing hold of Micheline, Mado swung her back and behind one of the pillars and then clutched her in a tight hug, whether to protect her or himself he was not quite sure. In any case there was no time for the niceties. Out of the corner of his eye he saw that the terrified Aziz had reduced himself into a small ball and had lodged himself on the marble floor in a corner.

'Mm!' Mado murmured, appreciating the aromatic scent Micheline wore, whilst at the same time wondering how best to control the wild flutter in his bladder. In contrast, though this only occurred to him when it was long over, the lady he was clutching in his arms seemed to be remarkably calm and poised.

'Keep your reactions to yourself,' Micheline whispered freeing herself with a slightly disdainful wriggle, 'you'll be needing your strength.'

That's as may be, he thought, but there was no time for further chat. A gunman in Phalangist uniform kicked open the door and strode into the hall, stopping dead when he saw Micheline, Mado and Aziz.

'So,' said the gunman to Aziz, 'it's you, Ulf Achmed.' The gunman nodded in approval at his own remark and then turned to Micheline. 'Madame Bariolet?'

'Yes.' This conversation was conducted in French. The gunman next turned slightly to George Mado.

'And you?'

'This is an Englishman,' Micheline said. 'What have you done? Have you killed my husband?'

'Before interrogation? Of course not. We are taking Monsieur Bariolet for questioning.'

'Are you sure he's all right?'

'Madame, we only kill enemies after a proper trial. When we know they are enemies. We are not idiot Palestinians. We are Phalangists.'

'Are you taking us, too?'

The gunman shook his head almost contemptuously.

'I advise you to go straight to the airport. It is still open if you can get there. Leave Beirut at once. You too,' he added, frowning at Mado, 'do not involve yourself here. All right, Ulf Achmed thank you for your help.'

Aziz had stood up and, was about to go to the door. The gunman shook his head.

'Stay here for ten minutes. Do nothing.'

Micheline moved towards the door and then at a threatening gesture from the gunman stopped.

'What are you going to do with my husband? I want to come too.'

'No, Madame. Do as I have just told you. Leave Beirut at once. The Syrians will soon be here. But there will be much trouble before they arrive. If Monsieur Bariolet tells us what we want to know, he will come to no harm.'

'I want to go with him. He needs looking after. He is not a young man.'

'I regret it, Madame, but no. See to it, Ulf Achmed.'

With a nod, the gunmen left and a moment or so later a car could be heard driving away at speed. The three looked at each other as the adrenalin seeped away in all of them.

'Well,' said Micheline, running her hands through her hair and looking around for a mirror, 'we had better make our way to the Clareville for a drink. I would also like to find out from Mr Aziz what Pemberton is up to these days. As perhaps you know,' she went on, shooting him a quizzical look and then beaming it on to Mado, 'as I'm *sure* you know, we have rather lost touch.'

George Mado and Micheline walked to the Clareville. She had invited Ulf Achmed Aziz to join them, but on leaving the house he suddenly vanished, melting away like a mirage in the desert. One moment he was there and the next he had gone. When he realised this had happened, Mado raised his eyebrows and made a gesture at Micheline which said, 'Well, it's just one of those things.' Micheline herself made no comment at all. She seemed to pay it no attention.

These days everyone went about Beirut on foot and generally kept counsel with themselves. A ceasefire would bring them all out in the streets, but ceasefires never lasted for long and it was said that Beirutis could smell the coming break of a truce much as a farmer can smell rain. Only terrorists, foreign embassies and the media had occasional access to wheeled transport, and such transport in any case remained in constant danger – as did anything that moved at speed – from the stray sniper's bullet.

As they walked Mado covertly observed his companion. It struck him that Micheline Bariolet seemed to be not only a highly attractive, vital woman who had clearly turned the tricky forties to her own advantage, but was also intensely and perhaps in the circumstances rather strangely self-possessed. He asked himself why she had reacted in so calm and unagitated a manner to the seizure of her husband by the Phalangists. It was almost as if she were expecting it, as if such an event had become an everyday experience.

Mado had had a lifetime's training in the art of observing people without it appearing either forced or obvious. He brought this faculty into play now as they picked their way through the rubble, keeping one eye open for the odd roving soldier or gang of terrorists and the other for the check-points which might or might not prove difficult to pass.

She was quite a hot number, as he would have described her in his youth. Everything about her bespoke money, but not in an aggressive way. From hair, perhaps a shade too blonde, to Gucci shoes, the signal was loud and clear that Micheline had accustomed herself to the use of great wealth for so long now that it had become second nature – which, in fact, was exactly what had happened.

Here was a very expensive lady indeed. He knew, of course, that Bariolet was the fourth millionaire she had married, and the built-in computer in Mado's head went to work to analyse what it was about a woman like Micheline that gave her the power over men such as Bariolet – a power which vibrated in her every movement, in her smile, in the scent she used and in the subtle way she seemed to flatter without this appearing to be obvious.

The sexual magnetism was deep, arresting and compulsive, yet instinctively he knew she could turn it off like a switch – or, perhaps more accurately, reverse the polarity. All sorts of warning bells began to sound in his brain. This was no dozy tart whose horizons were bounded by the yacht and the swimming pool. Instead the image of some powerful figure in history such as Catherine the Great arose in his mind. Meanwhile he masked his inner thoughts with a smile, and was amused to see that Micheline appeared to be doing the same whilst they carried on an easy exchange of trivial remarks about the pleasures of being out and about in a city like Beirut in the midst of a civil war.

One of the strange things about Beirut at that time was that, although power would be cut off or would otherwise fail for an increasing number of hours each day, the telephone system still worked, even if the crackling did remind its users of Edison Bell. When they reached the Clareville, therefore, and had been allowed to enter by a doorman whose function was clearly to prevent any stray Tom, Dick or Harry from availing themselves of the pre-crisis and still luxurious facilities within, Micheline put calls through to the police and then to some important politician – or so Mado gathered – reporting her husband's abduction to both.

'You make it sound like a routine event,' Mado suggested. She poured him a large Scotch from the well-stocked bar in the Bariolet suite. This, he had to admit, compared favourably with his own accommodation which consisted of one small room in a second-class doss-house near the embassy. Micheline then gave herself an equally large vodka on the rocks and curtly agreed.

'We pretend to be surprised, but to us and our friends this happens almost every day.'

'It can't do much for the tourist trade.'

'It's a game. At present both sides obey the rules. That Phalangist was right. If they discover what they want from Henri – or rather, if Henri tells them what he thinks they happen to want today – he'll be back here in a matter of hours. Of course things will change when the Syrians take over. But by then we shall have gone.'

'To Egypt?'

She shrugged her shoulders.

'We have houses in Cairo and Alexandria. Or Henri may decide to go to Athens.'

She looked at him in a smoky but calculating way. The bosom might be full and soft, the eyes appeared to have spikes. What was it Padstow had said about her? Mado tried to recall his briefing – the briefiest of briefings as it happened in so far as Madame Bariolet had been concerned, since at the time they had been concentrating on the great financier himself.

'The data bank has nothing on the lady which could possibly be of help to you, George; she's as clean as a whistle. Micheline Bariolet has never put a foot wrong, so far as we know. Nothing hostile – nothing provable at any rate. And yet, and yet there she is, always around. The only thing Records will commit on is that she does have questionable friends.'

'Who hasn't?' Mado had retorted. 'No doubt it keeps her amused.'

Mado never bothered to disguise the field operator's low opinion of what went on in Records.

'She's been around in a number of places and she's been

mixed up in events in which we *have* been interested, according to Records, but never with a direct connection of any kind. Heseltine Turk came across her in Egypt – or was it the Lebanon? – at the time of Operation Powder Train and all he could find to say was a quote out of Horace: "A beautiful woman is like a general: it takes a mishap to reveal his genius." And there's never been a mishap, so far as the data bank can tell.'

Well, of course, that was exactly the sort of remark Heseltine Turk would have been pleased to make. What Mado felt about Records could spread over to Heseltine Turk. Mado had been very much concerned with Operation Powder Train himself, and he had never been prepared to give the rather supercilious Heseltine Turk's opinion's a great deal of thought.

It was only afterwards that he remembered that Heseltine Turk had disappeared in mysterious circumstances very – but very – shortly after that particular operation, in fact when Mado himself had taken up a temporary residence in the Lubyanka Prison in Moscow. And nobody would tell him why. Perhaps nobody knew. Heseltine Turk was certainly a spy who had never come in from the cold, and Mado shivered slightly every time he remembered how many of them there had been. After Philby and Tarnham had defected, that is.

Ah well, there was not much point in tracking that particular train of thought. It was the longest of long shots to connect this gorgeously succulent lady with the disappearance of Heseltine Turk. Unless, of course, they had trained her as a sleeper for future use – but then on that basis, God knows, sleepers could be had for ten a penny.

'What brings you to Beirut, Mr Mado?'

'I thought you knew.'

'Perhaps I do. So why not confirm it?'

'I have a roving commission for Panayotis Marides.'

'And Mr Marides interests himself in Sheik Karim?

Together with – who were the Russians you mentioned? – General Karai and Andrei Simonov?'

'Well, it's the other way round, isn't it?' Mado said easily, noting that she was aware of General Simonov's first name. 'Simonov is the General, as I think you know, and all three are interested in Marides.'

'So?'

'So I would like to meet the Sheik, if you or Monsieur Bariolet would be so kind as to arrange it.'

'I am simply a banker's wife, Mr Mado. I never interfere. If my husband thinks you should meet the Sheik, no doubt you will.'

He was up against a ten-foot wall, and for a moment paused, wondering what next he should say.

He was saved from a decision by her asking, 'Tell me about your friend, Mr Aziz, who brought you to our house. I don't think I've met him before.'

'I shouldn't think you would have,' Mado answered with a sly grin, 'unless you happen to be active in the student drug scene. I knew him when I was last here in Beirut.'

'On Operation Powder Train?' Micheline said quietly. But there was a menace in her voice which made him freeze.

'You seem to be very well-informed.'

She brushed a piece of fluff from the emerald coloured slacks she was wearing.

'You know as well as the next man, Mr Mado, that international finance depends upon information. How else do you think my husband operates? Accurate, up-to-date news is the lifeblood of any business in Beirut.'

'Operation Powder Train scarcely comes into that category,' Mado said watchfully. 'All that was over in 1968.'

As he spoke the memory of his own abduction in the middle of the night came back to him, together with the subsequent spell he had spent in the prison when he had first met General Simonov.

Almost as if she were reading his thoughts, Micheline capped it by saying, 'Yes, all that is in the data bank, I've no doubt, but how do you suppose Mr Aziz knows my son Pemberton?'

'*I* have to tell *you*? I have to sing for my supper with that sort of information?'

'Of course you have to tell me. Whether that earns you another drink or not – that's something else.'

It crossed his mind that she was talking to him as if she had him covered with an invisible gun. At the same time the animal magnetism was such that it was all he could do to remain sitting in his seat.

'Your son Pemberton was by your third husband, the Swiss industrialist?'

'By my second. I'm not that old, Mr Mado.'

'I'm sorry. The "Mr Mado" bit is throwing me. Could it be George?'

'I'll think about it.'

'All right, then, by your second husband, Fuller, the Texan oil magnate. So Pemberton and his sister were brought up as Americans.'

'They are Americans – what else would you expect?'

'And when Pemberton was through with Harvard, you got Monsieur Bariolet to give him a job in the bank?'

She smiled. Suddenly it was as if the clouds had been whipped away by magic and she was a girl in a continental movie stepping out naked into the sunlight. Better watch yourself, sport, Mado said to himself, this one could be the death of you.

'I suppose you could put it that way. Actually a friend of ours in the State Department got him a quasi-diplomatic job connected with the American University of Beirut.'

'Which to anyone else would spell CIA.'

'If you want to be tedious.'

'So how is it you lost touch with your son?'

'Remember you're telling me, Mr Mado.'

'Here we go again.'

He was not at his best this morning. She was so obviously a magnificent lay and that was what he wanted to talk about, not her drippy son. It was on the tip of his tongue to ask how on earth she could put up with that bent old Lebanese banker who shared her bed. How could she do it? Money, money, money, he supposed. The root of all evil. Then he began to wonder who else had a bit on the side. He studied her glittering blue eyes and had the clear impression that she knew exactly what was going through his mind. She even smiled, as if to confirm it, just when he had reached that point in his private fantasy where he had got her into the shower and was kissing her passionately as the tiny jets of water needled down on to their skins.

'I think you've lost your train of thought, Mr Mado.'

'Not at all,' Mado said, ruffling up, but at the same time trying to remember what the hell he had been asking her. Pemberton – Pemberton Fuller, of course, that was what the dreary topic had been.

'Then your son got caught up with a Palestinian Marxist girl, didn't he,' Mado said, 'so he had to turn in the job and go underground?'

'I'm glad you're back on the beam,' she agreed. 'Yes, that's more or less the story. And do you know the girl?'

'No. How could I?'

'I think you do. She's had quite a career – and a number of names. You know two of them, and I think you gave her a third during that business in Rome – didn't you call her Miss Buttocks?'

'My God, Graziella-Ephrosini . . .' Mado said. 'You're right. She did have a magnificent arse.'

'There is no need to try and cover your surprise by being vulgar, Mr Mado.'

'Sorry,' Mado said, 'but you did take me by surprise. Yes,

she was quite a girl was Graziella-Ephrosini, a real killer bitch.'

'From all accounts she still is.'

Whilst Micheline refilled their glasses, Mado took his thoughts back to his previous visit to Beirut during the Powder Train operation. She had still been a left-wing student and he had seduced her on a lonely beach to the north of Beirut. Then, more recently, she had played a prominent part in the last PITO operation he had been concerned with. Graziella-Ephrosini was the archetype of the bejeaned girl guerrilla and she was very close to the PITO leadership – even to Mustafa Khaliq himself.

'So perhaps you can see how my son and I have lost touch with each other,' Micheline said, handing him his drink.

'I can see how it could be,' Mado said, which on reflection struck him as a double-edged remark. He was back in that shower again.

There was a slight pause as Micheline studied him over the rim of her glass.

'If I were you, George, I'd be careful not to ask too many questions here in Beirut these days. The legitimate business interests of that jumped-up Greek peasant are one thing; your old profession, another. Henri and I will be getting out just as soon as we can. I'd advise you to do the same.'

'Yes, I see what you mean.' Then suddenly, as if he had had an electric shock, 'Hey! didn't you call me George just now?'

'That's right, George, I did.'

She put down her glass, stood up and beckoned him across. Then she gave him one of the softest, most luscious, longest, lingering kisses he had ever experienced in what might be termed his labial life. Oh la la! he said to himself.

'Perhaps you'd better stay to lunch,' she murmured, taking his hand and leading him towards the bedroom. 'I don't know what we shall get but you'll be needing to keep up your strength.'

3

Andrea Eckersley returned to her room at the Cairo Hilton well pleased with the interview she had just completed. The President had been one of the more agreeable assignments, a 'nice' man in that peculiar classification the English still made, a man of destiny, sure of himself yet without any special aggression. There seemed to be few problems here and in her mind the profile had already begun to take shape. Other Arab leaders, such as those in Iraq and Libya, were unlikely to be so straightforward. But to hell with the morrow, she consoled herself, sufficient unto the day . . .

She was taking a shower when the telephone rang. Cursing the timing, she went into her bedroom and picked up the phone, catching sight of herself in the long mirror and instinctively tightening her tummy muscles.

'This is General Sayyid's ADC,' an educated voice said in English. 'The General would like to know if you could come to a small party he is giving at the Abakiya Palace tonight. Nothing formal. He understands you had a good meeting with the President and there will be one of two people he would like you to meet. He'll send a car for you, of course.'

She thanked the ADC and accepted the date. Social life in Cairo gave the impression of reverting to that of the bad old imperial days. Certainly the concern of most people centred once again on the making of money, and on what in post-war England would have been called 'rehabilitation'. Big American cars proliferated, and furniture shops were filled with that particularly hideous reproduction style known locally as 'Louis Farouk'.

She stood up to go back to the shower and then abruptly froze. She was not alone in the room. Absolutely still in a chair half hidden by the wardrobe sat a watchful, wary, George Mado. She snatched up the bedspread and draped herself angrily in it.

'You haven't lost your appalling bad taste,' she said. 'What the hell are you doing here?'

'How can it be bad taste to admire so beautifully proportioned a body as yours? Anyway, I knocked. But you were in the shower so I suppose you didn't hear.'

'So what? You've got a nerve.'

'Don't kick up like a prima donna,' Mado said with the glitter of a smile, 'just remember this isn't the first time I've sighted that magnificent Mons Andreatica – or have you forgotten? You gave me a short press conference in your bath in Athens when we were helping that dreary Greek Resident to slipper his way to the West.'

He saw the anger had begun to drain away in spite of herself.

'I apologise for taking you by surprise.' He blew her a kiss and then went on softly, 'I can only compound the felony by saying how delirious it would be to take you in a more conventional way.'

'You cheap little voyeur.'

But she was smiling and no longer bothered with the bedspread. 'Give me a cigarette and tell me what all this is about.'

Mado did as requested, kissing the firm rosy nipples *en route*. She did not seem to put up much opposition to this: there was evidently a measure of exhibitionism in her little ladyship. On the other hand, Mado thought, it's a bit like kissing a marble statue. Not that he did much of that.

'Naughty, naughty Mado!' she said, trying not to laugh out loud.

'We really ought to give it a whirl,' Mado said, pushing his luck, 'you do have one of the most ravishing torsos I've ever seen.'

'Yes, well, we won't take that any further,' she said briskly, and made a face at herself in the looking glass. 'Anyway, I'm supposed to be Miss Pillar of Ice, didn't you know?'

'Paf!' said Mado. 'I could do with a drink if you have a bottle stashed away in the cupboard.'

'I haven't, but I'll get you one.'

'No, don't!' Mado said urgently as she reached for the phone. 'The less obvious we are in our meetings the better. That's why I've broken in like this.'

'How *did* you get in, as a matter of fact?'

'If you're going to work for John Padstow on a long-term basis, my sweet, you must get him to give you the Boy's Own Very Special Outfit of pass keys for international hotels.'

'What's that about Padstow?' she said without thinking.

'Oh brace up, honey, you didn't *mean* that last question, did you? No, I thought not. Did you also forget young Master P. asking me to keep an eye on what you get up to out here? He may not have had this sort of scene in mind, it's true. Nevertheless Mado is here in line of duty.'

He was having to keep a heavy grip on himself as his eye kept soaking in, mostly with peripheral vision, the tawny red hair, the square shoulders, the slender hips, the almost boyish bottom and that superb triangular frontage, a delicate ginger in colour. After all, he asked himself, what was an elegant body there for if not to give pleasure to the eye?

'A gentleman is supposed to avert his gaze,' she said gently. 'Why don't you come to the point?'

'I'm trying to give it up – being a so-called gentleman, I mean. Oh yes, and coming to the point as well. What point?' He clicked his tongue and shot the ceiling a hopeless look. 'So okay! Business it is. You're about to have drinks with General Sayyid.'

She nodded.

'See what you can find out about a young Egyptian tiger called Captain, or he may be Major, Suleiman Masri. Like the President you've just been interviewing, he's a village boy made good. And he's a friend of Sayyid's son.'

'General Sayyid is no village boy.'

'Right. He's your old Ruling Class and Sandhurst trained. Sticks out like an old school tie at a comprehensive in the present governing cabal. However his son has friends in the required proletarian circles. That's what interests me – and a number of other people.'

'Why is General Sayyid in the scene at all?'

'If you've saved the life of a head of state not once but three times through nipping plots in the bud, you have a special position – however unfashionably right-wing your ideas may be, however un-working class the blood in your veins.'

'I think you're a snob, George Mado.'

'And who better to judge than yourself?'

The Venus of the bedspread walked into the shower, turned it off, and came back in a white towelling coat which made her look, if anything, more radiant than ever.

'Why are you so interested in Suleiman Masri?'

'There's something brewing which may come to the boil in a very short time – and Masri is something to do with it.'

'Another plot? Like we had in Rome?'

'Well, out here there's always a scheme on foot to assassinate someone or other. It's the why that's interesting. Also the real target, of course.'

'Do you know the real target yourself?'

Mado shook his head. 'Apart from that hardy perennial, the snatching of power. But the Commander of the Crossing – your actual President – is comparatively,' he dwelt hard on the word and then repeated it, 'comparatively safe from that stage of the game. If he hasn't achieved Nasserdom, he's got more going for him than anyone else in Egypt. There's always a chance of a palace revolution, of course, but there doesn't seem to be much popular support for that and General Sayyid the Protector is ever to hand.'

'Well then?'

'In certain directions our Russian friends can work to a time scale as long, as deep and as devious as the dear old Pope in the Vatican. They can wait. And they do. They've not done very well out here of late. Sadat threw them out. The Israeli situation is under control. That Libyan laughter-boy and his Iraqui friends can't pass their O-levels in international diplomacy. So what is Comrade Brush Off to do? Fancy being reduced to stirring it up in the Lebanon! Bit of a come-down, isn't it? Grade Z stuff, I'd say, and even the problems of the Suez Canal won't leak away into the desert. It's a gloomy outlook for the Arab lobby in the Kremlin these days.'

'Yes, yes,' Andrea said with an impatient toss of her head, 'I can do my own assessments for the popular press. So what's your line on the young Egyptian tiger?'

'I fancy it's much the same – though from the other side of the table – as it is on that well-known peripatetic Sheik, O Tarnham al What's-his-name. I'm told Masri is an activist – though in aid of what I just don't know. But there's something coming up that, from the Russian point of view, has got to be stopped. Some agreement, maybe, which they're not going to like. Kissinger isn't going to be there for ever. And it is US election year.'

'Hm,' said Andrea, thinking it out. She slipped out of the towelling robe, took a light linen dress of cornflower blue from the cupboard and with a deftness that would have done justice to a quick-change artiste made herself ready for the evening fray.

'How did you get on in Beirut?' She corrected herself, 'I should have said how did you get out of Beirut?'

'If you have a friend like Micheline Bariolet, you don't

need to worry too much about the fast cars and the helicopters.'

'And how did you make out with Madame?'

'In one respect better than I get on with you,' Mado said with a saucy grin, 'however – surprise, surprise – you I'd trust more.'

'That's the most idiotic remark you've made so far.' She looked at her watch. 'I think you'd better be on your way.'

'Yes,' Mado agreed with the trace of a sigh, 'see you around.'

He kissed her gently and deftly on the mouth, and then, almost before she had come to grips with that gesture, vanished from the room, the door barely clicking behind him. The telephone rang.

'Your car is waiting for you, madam,' the hall porter said.

There is little love lost between senior members of the KGB, any more than there is between rival Mafia units in the West. Gang morality applies – as it did in the Nazi SS – under the thin guise of discipline and loyalty to the holy tenets of the creed to which all are bound.

General Simonov and Colonel Karai, whom circumstances had thrown together many times before, detested each other and made scant effort to cover this up. Dissimilar in temperament, tastes and even in ambition, the two men met as infrequently as possible unless they found themselves in a situation, as they did now in Beirut, when a close working partnership had to be enforced. Each was correct, cold and contemptuous of the other.

Simonov had had a distinguished war career. By some miracle he had also survived the Stalin purges, so that he was of 'the old school' – if such a description could be applied to an organisation as baneful as the KGB.

Karai, who would have passed out top for Commandant

of a Nazi concentration camp, had developed into an apparatchik of the nuclear age, devoid of humanity but deadly accurate in his work. Now he was on the mat, an unusual state of affairs he did not relish at all.

'You say the Phalangists simply walked in and snatched our friend Bariolet? How did this happen? Who tipped them off?'

General Simonov glowered at his subordinate whom he had kept standing instead of treating to the usual cool formality of asking him to be seated.

'The man's name is Ulf Achmed Aziz; Arab father, Swedish mother, club organiser, hanger-on in student circles at the American University, experienced in the distribution of drugs, a known double agent but none the less useful where he is.'

'Useful to whom? Not now to us.'

Karai shrugged his shoulders and looked scornfully at the picture on the desk of the General being decorated by the Head of State.

'That is not for me to say. Our local Resident speaks highly of the work he has done in the past. A double agent in the nature of things works for at least two masters, both of whom may be aware of the fact.'

'I do not require a lecture on field work, Colonel Karai. Where is our banker now?'

'We do not know.'

'Then find out and have him brought here.'

'Easier said than done.'

'I dare say. Nevertheless do it. You claim Mado was there at the time? Better bring him in, too.'

'He left almost as once for Cairo with Madame Bariolet.'

'With?'

'In her company,' Karai said, still zoning a ray of icy dislike at his more easy-going superior.

'Are you telling me she's also a double agent?'

'I have no knowledge of that. I very much doubt it, however. She's not an agent at all. She's simply married to Henri Bariolet.'

'She is also the mother of Pemberton Fuller.'

Karai nodded briefly and said nothing. He had no idea what the old fool would say next. He was glad he had been able to have a private word with the man known as Sheik Karim al Hammad before he had flown back to Moscow the previous night. He did not think the late defector from the British Foreign Service, who had been put in over-all command of this current operation, to the surprise and dislike of the regular KGB operatives in the area, had much use for the ageing General Simonov.

Karai had suggested over the farewell vodkas (and Karai only used alcohol when required to do so on duty) that Simonov was getting too worn-out for the job. He'd been working too hard, of course. Perhaps he would soon be ready for the shelf, Karai had murmured, and Tarnham (or the Sheik) had given him that malicious smile and quick nod which gainsaid the cold formal retort haughtily given that such matters were not in the purview of the Sheik's present responsibilities. A nod and a smile did not get recorded on tape. Both men were practised in the double-think, double-talk techniques which alone spell survival in the Marxist world. No doubt the poison would filter through and do its work in the right department at No. 2 Dzerzhinsky Square. Karai had not studied Himmler's career for nothing. He could wait.

'What is to be done with the double agent Aziz?' he asked.

'I'll decide that when we've recovered Bariolet. That must be the first priority. Without Bariolet in financial control, the operation could well be delayed or endangered. These Palestinian peasants have still got to be paid.'

'Is there no contingency plan?' Karai asked, knowing full well that such a question would never be answered whilst the recording machine in the General's drawer was still switched on. General Simonov stared at his subordinate in a nasty way.

'There is very little time left,' he said, and jerked his head at the door. Outside the embassy a fresh rumble of gunfire could be heard. The Syrians were moving nearer.

The Cairo Hilton is a convenient centre for residents and visiting firemen to meet, whether from business, diplomacy or the media. Communications are passable for Egypt, and it is but a step to the Gezira Club in one direction over the Tahir bridge, and to the heart of commercial Cairo in the other towards Al Azhar Square. Lars Sweeney, who believed in blending pleasure with his work to the maximum degree possible, had spent a hot afternoon at the races at Gezira and had been hoping to take Andrea to dinner at one of the restaurants overlooking the Nile.

'It says here,' he told Andrea on the telephone when making the date earlier in the day, 'that "night-time in Cairo combines the magic of the East with the arts of the West to offer the visitors a night life brimful with every type of enjoyment and beauty." How about that? So why not brim it up with me once you're through with your presidential assignment?'

Andrea had agreed. As a result Lars had been looking forward to it right through the tedious and heavy calculations he had been forced to make at the racecourse that afternoon.

He was, therefore, somewhat put out when she did not appear on time in the Hilton bar and he found himself instead having a drink with Pemberton Fuller, who had sent a message that he would like to see him in a hurry. Lars had been warned about Pemberton Fuller. Not that this made much difference. Lars had reached that stage in life when, whatever the briefing, he made up his own mind on people and events. So far as Pemberton Fuller was concerned, Lars was neutral.

Pemberton Fuller might have something useful to say. On the other hand he might not. What did it really matter?

He slipped away the brief note Andrea had sent him saying that she would have to attend General Sayyid's party and therefore might be a little late. A little late indeed! He had heard that one before. What he was not prepared to accept was comment from this tubby, dark young man with the restless eyes whom he had never met before. Mr Pemberton Fuller, ex-CIA.

'She's stood you up?'

Lars Sweeney took in the shifty eyes and the slight leer, and held the pause for as long as it pleased him.

'You wanted to see me, Mr Fuller?'

'Sure I wanted to see you. Otherwise why are we here? I was commenting on that message you just received.'

'Well, how about that?' Lars said lightly enough.

'She *has* stood you up?'

'Mr Fuller, I don't know what you're talking about. Which "she" do you have in mind?'

'That glamorous red-headed newspaper woman who's here to see the President.'

'Oh her!' Sweeney said, studying his drink. 'Yes, she's an attractive girl.'

Lars Sweeney was an old hand at this particular game. He relapsed into silence, apparently lost in his thoughts. He was not minded to help this young man in any way. Pemberton Fuller struck him as the sort of pushy fellow who, at Harvard, would have been dubbed a 'Tuft Hunter'. Privately he was surprised that Fuller had made Harvard at all.

'You're right, Lars,' Pemberton Fuller went on (and who gave him permission to call him Lars?) 'There's no doubt she is a highly attractive girl. General Sayyid undoubtedly has an eye for a bit of tail.'

'For what?' Sweeney said, suppressing a shudder. 'Ah yes, I see what you mean . . .'

'However, don't let's waste time. I think we both know what Lady Andrea Eckersley is interested in.'

This – it struck Lars – was a brave, maybe even a desperate, attempt to get to the point at once. As a throwaway remark it might well have worked, but Pemberton Fuller was so obviously in a highly nervous state that it merely sounded like an amateur actor reading lines he did not understand.

'That's a whole lot more than *I* know,' Lars Sweeney eventually said. 'In what way are we wasting time? It's a fine evening. You asked for this meeting. So go ahead – ask any questions you want.'

'Don't lose your cool.' Pemberton Fuller tried to keep the anxiety out of his voice and failed. 'Simple loyalty to the old firm induces me to pass on a warning, that's all.' Lars Sweeney studied him in silence and eventually, without further encouragement, Fuller went on, 'Nothing personal, of course, but I'm sure you'll direct it to where it matters . . .'

Sweeney continued to stare at him without opening his mouth. His legal training had long ago taught him how effective such silent non-reaction could be.

'Well . . .' Fuller faltered a little, 'what I mean is I should be very careful about any approach you may receive on . . . as to what Andrea Eckersley wants to know.'

'Is that the extent of the message?' Sweeney asked, taking a long slow pull at his drink.

'I don't have to remind an experienced man like yourself that Cairo of all places is a hotbed of false information. I . . . I . . .'

'Tell me, Mr Fuller, what is it that makes you so scared.'

'How's that?'

'You're certainly under pressure. I take it you're also under surveillance. Are you being watched at this moment?'

'This is just crazy. What's all this about "surveillance" and "being watched"? Look, I'm simply trying to pass on a warning, that's all. Just be careful, that's all I'm trying to say.'

At that moment George Mado appeared at the far end of the room, and with a quick flick of his head Lars Sweeney asked him across.

'This is Pemberton Fuller,' Sweeney said, brushing some imaginary scurf off the collar of his coat.

'Ah,' said Mado, shaking hands and giving the paunchy young man one of his twisted smiles, 'now that's nice!'

'You know each other?'

'I know *of* Mr Mado, of course.'

'Like who doesn't in the great *demi-monde* of Intelligence?' Mado said with false grandiloquence. Then he turned to Sweeney. 'Thank you, Lars, I'll take a large malt whisky on the rocks since you were kind enough to ask. What brings you to Cairo, Mr Fuller? I thought your manor was the Lebanon.'

'Mr Fuller wishes to warn us,' Sweeney said, 'though exactly what about, I couldn't quite discover.'

'Ah,' said Mado, 'now that's nice, too! We've been a bit slack in the warning department of late. Oh, yes. Ho, ho, hum!'

A silence fell between the three of them. Mado's internal calculating machine had quietly begun to flash up the danger code. Micheline Bariolet's son by her second marriage bore little resemblance to his glamorous mother. He was not as pretty for a start, and then he had this habit of furtively looking over his shoulder. He seemed to exude the sort of seedy insecurity more appropriate to someone selling goods that have fallen off the back of a truck. Not a man you would guess had had a Texan oil tycoon for a father. Ho – ho – hum, indeed!

'I met your mother in Beirut,' Mado said, breaking the silence and examining his drink.

'I know.'

'Ah!' said Mado. He was becoming rather fond of saying 'Ah!' when he had nothing else to remark.

'Why did you engineer the snatching of Monsieur Bariolet?' Pemberton Fuller enquired. 'That was not a friendly act.'

'I don't suppose it was. But then you have to ask – friendly to whom? In any case why go for me? That snatch had nothing to do with me. You know that perfectly well.'

'Poor Ulf Achmed Aziz,' the young Texan went on, 'he was for so long a part of the scene. We all took him for granted.'

'Well, he was handy for the hash, was he not?'

'That and other things. Not a good way to end, though, was it?'

'Ah!' said Mado, this time giving the sound an almost lyrically reflective note. 'I didn't know his end had come.'

'The guy shot himself through the mouth, blowing off the top of his head. They found his body yesterday on a beach. Can't have been a pleasant sight. But then a whole raft of unpleasant things go on in Beirut these days. It's a dangerous part of the world.'

'What are you trying to warn us about, Mr Fuller? You must be aware that I'm no longer in the security game any more than you are yourself. I believe you and the CIA parted company some time ago – am I right? So we're both in private practice, so to speak. I don't know who or what you work for and I wouldn't be so rude as to ask. But I work for Marides now – and so does Lars Sweeney here. What warning are we to pass on to the great Panayotis?'

'If I were you, Mr Mado, I'd make an excuse and catch the next flight home. Cairo can be just as unhealthy as Beirut. Things are done more quietly here, that's all.'

Pemberton Fuller became the target for two pairs of hard, unfriendly eyes.

'What things did you have in mind?'

They were not giving him an easy time. Indeed Pemberton Fuller's attempt at a threat seemed to be so amateur as to be laughable – which was in itself a matter of suspicion. Had he been a thug with a gun standing over them in some dank cellar, Pemberton Fuller's behaviour might just have made sense. In the bar of the Cairo Hilton all that was being achieved appeared to be a state of creeping incredulity.

'You know what I'm talking about, Mr Mado.'

'Possibly,' Mado said, watching him in a clinical fashion, 'and then again, possibly not. On the other hand *I* might ask *you* if *you* know what *you're* talking about. What's screwing you up, Mr Fuller? And talking of screwing – how's Graziella these days?'

This was a deliberately offensive remark which had the desired effect. It made Pemberton Fuller angry.

'Get screwed yourself,' he said, and abruptly left. Mado and Sweeney looked at each other and then let their eyes follow the departing figure as it strode angrily – and somewhat podgily – out of the bar.

'I don't think that was quite as inept and ingenuous as the little fellow intended it to be,' Mado said, looking carefully round the room. 'Why am I getting that old old shiver back of the spine? Who is it who has us lined up in his sights? Or am I just being a silly old moo?'

'I doubt it,' Sweeney said, 'I'm getting that feeling too.'

Gently Mado put down his glass.

'See you the nonce,' he said, and slipped out of the bar so quickly and attracting so little attention that the two separate men who were watching the scene did not realise he had gone until he had vanished.

General Ismat Sayyid turned out to be almost exactly the sort of man Andrea had expected him to be. Tall, not over-paunched and possessed of an erect, military bearing as befitted a Sandhurst-trained officer of the old school, he wore his impeccable uniform with its four rows of medals in an almost jaunty fashion, and his eyes, Andrea decided, might well be described as 'crinkled with experience', the little creases on either side caused no doubt by incessant study of a desert horizon through binoculars. He had an elegance and a charm which she had found conspicuously lacking in the new generation of jumped-up captains and majors.

How, she wondered, had he survived the Nasser regime? She marked down this question in her mind for asking after a better acquaintance.

In fact, General Sayyid had had remarkably little to do with front-line warfare, but a great deal to do with the training of others and the procurement of military supplies. He had made himself into a highly skilled negotiator not only with the British, the Americans and the French but also, surprisingly, with the Russians, and this perhaps had been the principal reason he had not been axed after the overthrow of Farouk.

As a result of these skills he had also become a wealthy man, but his deep and continuing reading of history led him to be on his guard against greed. The endemic corruption of Egypt in particular and the Middle East in general, therefore, did not trouble him to any dangerous extent. There is no one in that world who is not corrupt to a degree, since the kick-back is a way of life, but Sayyid had long ago learnt to be shrewd enough never to put himself at the head of the queue.

Certainly the numbered account in Zurich grew steadily – it is necessary from time to time to water the flowers, as the French say – but the accretion of Swiss francs and dollars came about almost as an afterthought to any deal, and there had never been any danger of this intermittent process becoming a matter of scandal. After all, his father had been a wealthy man and his mother, who was a Greek-Egyptian, had been a considerable heiress in the old imperial days.

All this had induced an ease of manner which was deceptive. Behind the smile, behind the physical attractiveness of a powerful man, behind the well-bred consideration of others, especially if they happened to be women, lay a sharp intelligence and a very determined will.

'I am told you made a good impression on the President,' he said to Andrea when they were able to have a word together *à deux*, 'I hope it will show in the finished result.'

'You wouldn't be trying to pre-empt that result with Dom Perignon?' Andrea replied, a little smile round her lips.

'Of course I am. Let me get you another glass.'

She shook her head and then said on the spur of the moment, 'I might do a piece about *you* when the time is right.'

It was a casual remark, meant as light flattery but without overtones. She was therefore surprised to see a sudden flash which came and left his eyes so rapidly she would have missed it had she not been looking at him directly.

'I'm just a backroom boy,' he said lightly, 'I don't think your public would be interested in an old hanger-on like me.'

'Survival is fascinating in itself – if that doesn't sound rude.'

'My dear lady, you couldn't be rude to a professional survivor such as myself. Not with a remark like that. You should meet some other members of the press who pass through our hands.'

'I have done,' Andrea said, 'we're a pretty unlovely lot.'

'It's a pretty unlovely job.'

'We have our rewards.'

'I shall be interested to see how you get on next door.'

'I take it you mean Libya and not Israel by that jerk of the head.'

The General smiled, 'Surely Israel doesn't come into your terms of reference?'

'It could do. I have a free hand. But I think I'll confine myself to the Arab world.'

'Well,' General Sayyid said, looking into the distance, 'it will make no difference to us. Although I imagine the President would prefer you to keep it the way it is – but, as you say, that's entirely your own affair. I'll add this though. If you are going to Tripoli in the near future, my son may be able to help. Relations at our level – the President's and mine – are still necessarily cool, but my son knows one or two people you might like to meet.'

'Your son is in Security?'

'For want of a better word, yes.' He looked at her with a slightly bantering smile. 'We have to keep a weather eye on our Boy Scout neighbours. I'm sure I needn't expand on that.'

Andrea nodded and looked across the marble-floored reception room at a small knot of Egyptian officers of the younger generation.

'That's your son over there?'

The General nodded.

'He's with another young officer you should meet. Major Masri – one of our Heroes of the Crossing.'

You could not talk long to Egyptians without some reference to the 1973 war, Andrea reflected, and dead boring it usually turned out to be. However, as the victory over Israel remained the key fact conditioning the whole of the present day Middle Eastern scene, this had to be accepted. After all, the President was universally known in the vernacular as 'The Commander of the Crossing'.

'Major Masri has an interesting face,' Andrea remarked casually as the General led her across.

'Oh yes, indeed! In the old days his confidential report would have given him ten out of ten for powers of leadership and other officer-like qualities. Not bad for a boy whose father was one of the fellaheen. From the next village to where the President was born, as a matter of fact. But that's the age we live in, Lady Andrea, is it not? Oh! Micheline,' he broke off to speak to a woman with whom it was at once obvious he was on friendly terms, 'this is Andrea Eckersley from London. Have you any news of Henri?'

Micheline and Andrea nodded at each other, acknowledging the introduction, and then Micheline said, 'No good news, I'm afraid. Your crazy Phalangists are holding him as a hostage.'

'They are certainly not *my* Phalangists,' the General said with the first touch of sharpness he had exhibited. 'What on earth put that idea in your head?'

'It's so difficult to get a rise out of General Sayyid,' Micheline remarked to Andrea, 'but often worth while if you can.'

Then they gave each other the appraising look of two people who have been told a certain amount about each other but who were meeting for the first time.

'I'm so glad to have met you at last,' Micheline said, and winked before turning away.

4

Later in the party, in fact just when people were beginning to leave, Andrea found Micheline Bariolet at her side once more.

'If you're not going on to dinner,' Micheline said, 'perhaps you might like to come back with me. We can either have something to eat at home, or there's a new place I want to try out where the air conditioning works even if the food is not all that remarkable, which I'm afraid it's not.'

The two women studied each other in the smiling, civilised way that ambassadors adopt when they talk to their counterparts in countries which are non-aligned but not necessarily hostile to each other. The verbal exchange was easy, and yet underneath, it struck Andrea, there were still vibrations of some undefined threat. Or was her imagination running away with her in an irresponsible way? She had felt the same thing with General Sayyid, for all his elegant good manners, and it annoyed her not to be able to pinpoint the cause.

'I'd love to,' Andrea said, remembering her date with Lars and then putting it out of her mind. She had become subtly intrigued, both as a writer and as a woman, by this graceful, poised creature who had started life as skinny little Rita Morgan of Swansea, one of the countless Morgans of that treeless, unlovely port, and who had made it via four rich, rich husbands to this baroque palace on the banks of the Nile.

Micheline struck her as a very finished lady who was in no way finished, and Andrea was amused by the slight French accent. She supposed it to be entirely simulated and at the same time she realised that Micheline cared not a fig that this must be obvious. So what did she care a fig about? It might be interesting to find out.

Micheline, indeed, gave the impression of being entirely sure of herself without the blemish of aggression. From the way those clear blue eyes could suddenly flash, though, Andrea realised that there must be a pressure of temper in the woman which might make her spit like a cat if occasion required it.

Suppressing a feeling of slight envy, Andrea sensed the sexual basis of this power, recognising that she herself still inhabited a sexual no-man's-land in spite of the advantages she had enjoyed from her own more aristocratic start in life. Ah well, she consoled herself, she might not succeed in the sack with such practised ease, but on the other hand Micheline could never have the satisfaction which her column in the Sundays gave her.

Abruptly she broke her train of thought: each of them had reached the top of a separate tree and there was no point in trying to judge which gave the more satisfying view.

'How did you make out with our young Hero of the Crossing?' Micheline asked, as they sat in her Mercedes driving towards the Nile and the Bariolet mansion. 'Major Masri, I mean.'

'He hasn't much use for women, has he?'

'Apart from the crude and obvious ones, no. His proletarian mores remain obstinately nonconformist – even today when everyone in Egypt is *so* emancipated,' the light sarcasm did not strike Andrea as bitter but simply as a passing comment on the scene, 'the threat of the yashmak still hangs over us all,' Micheline went on, 'and sometimes this can even be turned to advantage, although it might take me some time to explain what I mean. You get a feeling about it, though, if you live out here for any length of time.'

Andrea had the writer's ability to take a dive out of her

own consciousness and surface invisibly in that of the person she was with. Micheline was driving with a firm decisiveness through the bustling night-time traffic of Cairo, but there seemed to be a slight incongruity in the statement she had just made, or rather in the words she had used. Or was it a hesitation, as if she were trying something out?

'He talked about Libya,' Andrea said. 'He didn't seem to think I'd get very far along that particular road.'

'I'm surprised you're being allowed in there at all.'

'Well, it's the media magic, isn't it?' Andrea commented with her tongue in her cheek. 'You'd be surprised what people will do to keep in with the new orthodoxy. Even Major Masri unbent as I worked a little of the poison into his system. Those "real men" are the easiest of all. Underneath they're fascinated by what the press and the telly can do for their flashy ambitions. Although I admit I didn't get far on that score with Masri. I take it he *is* ambitious?'

'You already know more about him than I do,' Micheline said, parrying the question as they turned into the grounds of the Bariolet house. It was casually said, yet it scarcely rang true. 'What sort of things are you trying to find out?' she asked as she stopped the car in front of an imposing set of steps leading to an equally imposing front door.

'Well, for a start, why did General Sayyid suggest that I meet him?'

Micheline looked slightly surprised. She paused before answering and then, shrugging her shoulders, passed off the question lightly enough.

'I imagine he was trying to help you with some of your non-Egyptian problems.'

Yes, Andrea thought, it could be that, but there was something about Micheline's manner which put her more than ever on her guard. They left the car for a servant to garage, walked up the steps to the front door, which opened silently in front of them, and then walked through a cool, marble hall with a wide winding staircase to a softly lit terrace overlooking the Nile. A silent houseman in the usual white sheeting followed at a respectful distance, and when they were seated on the wicker chair took their orders for drinks with a small, dignified bow. This was a very grand establishment indeed, Andrea concluded, almost as imperial as the palace of General Sayyid.

'Of course, I'm sure you realise General Sayyid is no fool,' Micheline said when they had settled themselves. 'In the Middle East it's never wise to isolate yourself for any length of time: keep in with all areas of intelligence and information, however important a man you are. Sayyid's son and his son's friends will filter him news he might not get in any other way. Egypt is a land of intrigue. No one can be safe who sits back and expects life to go on tomorrow as it does today. Least of all the President and General Sayyid.'

'The General struck me as a womaniser,' Andrea remarked. She felt herself having to resist, and at the same time was finding herself alert and privately astonished by the magnetism which Micheline seemed to be beaming her way.

'Not a very deep observation,' Micheline retorted, but without a biting edge, 'name me one Egyptian of his wealth and standing who isn't. They all have wives of an arresting ugliness.'

'With hearts of gold?'

'I'm not so sure about that. They may be of Nile mud for all I know.'

A silence fell between them as they looked out at the dark garden, the palm trees ruffling slightly in the breeze. It was almost a standard setting for sexuality of some kind, and Andrea was amused by the notion that such an event might be in the offing. Romantic vibrations seemed to be buzzing about like a swarm of contented bees.

'Why are you smiling?' Micheline asked.

Andrea looked at her nails and decided to risk it. 'I was wondering what you had in mind.'

'We were talking about General Sayyid,' Micheline replied, quickly switching ideas, 'and in Cairo seduction is in the air we breathe. However, what *I* was wondering was what it really is that Marides wants you to find out or do on this trip.'

'Marides?' Andrea said, her astonishment for the moment holding at bay the uneasy threat she was beginning to sense. 'I'm not working for Marides. What put that idea in your mind?'

'You saw him just before you came out here.'

'And last year I saw the Pope and the President of the United States. I wasn't working for them either.'

'Why are you and your friends Sweeney and Mado so anxious to meet Sheik Karim al Hammad?'

Andrea played it as coolly as she knew how, which, in fact, she was well practised in doing.

'I can't speak for my "friends", as you call them. Me?' She shrugged her shoulders. 'I'm not especially concerned to get together with the Sheik, as you seem to think. I met him in London before coming out here.'

'I know. He told me.'

Andrea stared woodenly at what she had to admit was a lovely, brown-skinned thigh, the split skirt allowing it to be seen right up to where the tiny briefs were just, but only just, containing the dark pubic hair. However, the sexual wavelength suddenly began closing down, and a much more sinister one seemed to be taking its place. Outside in the garden the cicadas kept up their endless whirring, except for short dramatic breaks during which the total silence produced an exaggerated effect.

'Your Intelligence friends suspect that something is going to happen out here,' Micheline said quietly, 'and they may well be right. Something usually does happen out here – and even more so in Beirut. But as to what that might be, I know as little or as much as you do.' She paused and then added softly, 'But if I were you I should stick to the scribbling. That way you'll be safe.'

'Thanks for the advice. Do all your guests get treatment like this?'

'No,' Micheline smiled, 'you're special. Very special indeed.'

The seduction channel had opened up again and now Andrea decided to face it head on.

'I'm always fascinated . . .' Andrea began, and then paused for the right words.

'I'm glad the message is getting through.'

'I don't know that it is. What message, if it comes to that?' Micheline looked away and did not reply, so Andrea went on, 'Who told you to talk to me like this?'

'Oh! I don't get told to do things. Not after four husbands. I usually do the telling.'

Very well, Andrea thought, if that's the way it's going to be we'd better come straight to the point.

'I see,' she said, 'then let me ask you another question – a little more to the point: are you the sleeper in this operation?'

The unexpected use of this trade word in Intelligence caused Micheline to become very still. Now the eyes were watchful and calculating. A long pause ensued.

'So you are what they said you were,' Micheline murmured in the end.

'I don't know what that means,' Andrea said. She felt rightly or wrongly that she had somehow or other regained the initiative. 'I have friends who write spy thrillers, that's all. I keep my eyes open for any good plots there may be lying around. Those are the only operations I'm interested in.'

'Of course,' Micheline agreed in a husky voice and rose to her feet in a sinuous way. 'Now let's go and have some food – and develop our literary ideas. You deserve to be fed.'

Perhaps I do, perhaps I don't, Andrea thought. She was not at all sure how long she could put up with the glamorous Madame Bariolet and all this clobber by the Nile.

A lifetime of being watched, of keeping an eye on others and generally of getting it together behind the Iron Curtain had given Mado a master's degree in throwing followers off the scent, not only in the more complicated civilised cities of the West, but also in neutral, or at least non-hostile, places such as Cairo.

On leaving the Hilton, therefore, in pursuit of Pemberton Fuller, he had no difficulty in sloughing off his own surveillance, whilst keeping a close eye on the pudgy little Texan. Old age pensioner though he nearly was, Mado still took pleasure in exercising one or two small but essential skills. Invisible he could never be, but he did possess a chameleon quality both in movement and in adaptation to the particular environment in which he had to work. One moment he was there and the next he was not. Thus Pemberton Fuller never appreciated that his meeting in one of the sleazier bars near the Souk with Graziella and another Palestinian girl terrorist had been overseen by Mado. Nor for that matter did Graziella herself.

The meeting in the bar wasted almost no time at all and all three then got into a car driven by a gorilla whom Mado took to be another Palestinian from the heavy brigade. Following in a taxi, Mado saw them into a quiet house on the road to the Pyramids, noted the location and then decided he had sleuthed enough for one evening. Now he needed to relax.

'Where does the effendi wish to go next?' his taxi-driver asked, and before Mado could answer embarked on the usual verbal sales effusion which gives Egyptian taxi drivers their charm. 'Effendi take moonlight visit to Pyramids? Abdul qualified guide.'

'Do I look like a man in need of a moonlight trip to the Pyramids?' Mado began, and then realised that the taxi-driver's command of English was unlikely to extend to irony. A better answer would be the word he used next.

'No,' he said, 'but thank you all the same.'

'Touristic hotel with full modern equipment?' Abdul pressed on hopefully. 'Nice girls?'

'Ah,' said Mado, 'that's more like it! But first – do you know the Al Fayoum Club?'

This question produced an unexpected reaction. Abdul first of all went rigid and then turned round to stare at Mado.

'How do you know about the Al Fayoum Club?' he asked in Russian, a question and a language which for a second or two left Mado nonplussed.

'I have a Maltese friend in Rome,' Mado eventually replied, also in Russian, 'he runs the Sanctuary Club, as it happens, and he said if ever I went to Cairo I should visit the Club Al Fayoum. How come you speak Russian? And how did you guess I speak it myself?'

'We had them in Egypt,' Abdul said, deflecting the query. 'I thought perhaps the effendi was a Comrade when he asked for the Club Al Fayoum.'

'I see,' Mado said, which meant that he didn't. He supposed the Club Al Fayoum must be where they all went.

'What is your occupation, effendi?'

'Look, Abdul,' Mado reverted to English, 'I'm sitting in your cab and I'm doing the paying. Leave the questions to me. I know all taxi-drivers report their interesting fares to the Ministry of Security.'

'To the police.'

'To the Ministry of Security. So, of course, you will be reporting me. This will not astonish the Egyptian State Security. My name is George Mado and my photograph and curriculum vitae are on file in every Ministry of the Interior in every country in Europe and the Middle East. What about you?'

'Effendi, I am a simple taxi-driver and guide.'

'Who speaks Russian.'

'And English.'

'And English very much better than when I first sat in this cab.'

Abdul laughed.

'We all have to earn a living. How can I be of use?'

'That's better,' Mado said, 'we're beginning to understand each other. Do you happen to know the people I was following out here?'

'Everyone in Cairo knows Pemberton Fuller, effendi. The CIA threw him out because he sleeps with a Palestinian girl.'

'Graziello-Ephrosini.'

'Aywah. A dangerous lady.'

'A terrorist, Abdul, a cool buttocky killer.'

'I see from the way the effendi speaks that he has a previous knowledge of Signorina Graziella-Ephrosini.'

'Aywah to you, Abdul. But all that is far in the past – in Beirut.'

There was a slight pause. Then the taxi-driver continued in a harder tone of voice, 'They should go back to Beirut. These people are not for Egypt.'

'We'll keep off the politics, Abdul.'

'As the Pasha decides.'

'At what point do I become a Sultan?' Mado asked.

'We Egyptians have long Turkish memories,' Abdul said, but now he was smiling and although Mado realised it might be inadvisable to trust him further than he could see, the situation seemed to be improving. 'The effendi works for MI5?'

'No longer,' Mado said, as truthfully as he could manage, 'and it's no longer MI5. No, Abdul, the effendi has retired. However, certain interests remain. Whose house have

Pemberton Fuller and his PITO girlfriend gone into?' As Abdul did not seem disposed to answer at once, Mado went on, 'You know that I can and will find that out without a great deal of trouble.'

'It is the house of Major Suleiman Masri, one of our Heroes of the Crossing.'

'Ah yes,' Mado said, feeling as if he had been forced to brake hard on an icy road, 'the October war . . . Suppose we go and have a drink at the Al Fayoum?'

Abdul started the engine.

'I will take the effendi where he wishes,' he said, 'but I shall not be able to accept your hospitality. It is forbidden for a camel-driver to leave his camel when he is on duty.'

'And this taxi is your ship of the desert?'

'How well the effendi understands!' Abdul said as they set off once more for the centre of Cairo. By the time they reached the Club Al Fayoum, Abdul had almost totally re-gained the pidgin English in which he had first chosen to con-verse. The fare demanded was almost three times what the tariff said it should be. Ah well, Mado consoled himself, you had to pay through the nose for anything of the slightest value these days.

'I like you, Abdul,' Mado said, 'how can I hire you again?'

'Take my card, effendi. If Allah so wills our paths will cross again.'

'I was wondering when Allah would get into the act,' Mado said, and found his way into the Club Al Fayoum which, like its counterpart in Rome, had been situated in a basement to which, it seemed, there were several entrances and exits.

In every major capital city, both in the West and in the Middle East, there is at least one foyer where spies, agents and other operatives whose work normally takes them into the shadowy back streets of Security can meet on safe ground without fear of traps, bugging devices and the rest of the paraphernalia cluttering up their daily lives. In other words, a sanctuary of sorts has to exist.

Indeed, in Rome the club in question is actually called Il Santuario. Usually these meeting places are run by Mafia or para-Mafia characters who have an understanding with the police and the Security Services of the host city. They are tolerated, even encouraged, for one obvious reason – it is better to know where people are.

These meeting places are not available to the casual tourist or visitor, and when by accident such people stray into their precincts, they find themselves tactfully ushered on their way after some courtesy hospitality from the management. Obviously no written rules exist, but in each club of this kind the 'members' rely on one simple but universally observed custom – they will be free from molestation, arrest or harassment so long as they are on the premises. Fate may lurk in wait outside in the street: it will never strike in the club itself.

The deeply protected working operative will naturally avoid such places. To set foot in Il Santuario in Rome, or in the Club Al Fayoum in Cairo, is to declare your identity if not your purpose. But thirty years after the ending of World War II the Security and Intelligence words are littered with known spies whose usefulness may not have entirely leaked away through being revealed for what they are. These people all have their place.

George Mado had been blown in the mid-sixties when Tarnham had defected, but he continued to be of use if only as a stool pigeon, although initially this had not been a role he especially relished. 'However sport,' he would declare, 'we all come to terms with our lives or we perish.' In fact, these days, Mado rather enjoyed being known for what he was. It gave him a cachet – perhaps even protection of a kind, since the

KGB was no longer disposed to bother itself too much with the work-horses of the past.

Occasionally, if the current operation happened to be more than usually tricky or delicate, Mado would find himself removed from the scene and leant upon for a time, but nowadays even this never lasted for long. They've squeezed this particular lemon dry, he would announce, so what's the purpose of breathing so heavily on me now? 'You don't breathe heavily on lemons' it would be pointed out to him, to which Mado retorted 'What the hell?'

This outlook might not always be shared by the front men of the hostile element, and certainly the really hard ones, such as Colonel Karai, would have preferred Mado out of the way, a victim of some standard accident. Killers always thought like that – was it not always cleaner to kill? – and Mado was never unwise enough to overlook that attitude for long. In the meantime, however, and with a wary eye in the back of his head, Mado continued to keep as many balls in the air as he could. The show must go on – or some such idiotic cliché. So now he walked up to one end of the bar in the Club Al Fayoum and asked for a large malt whisky, if they had such a thing.

'Welcome to Cairo, Mr Mado,' the barman said, 'I think we have the brand you like.'

'Well, well, well,' Mado said, 'things are looking up on this side of the Nile.'

'As indeed they are on the other,' the barman said. 'We were wondering when you would pay us a call.'

Mado decided to igonore the slightly disturbing undertone he seemed to detect. The barman, disguised in the obligatory white gallabia, appeared to be a typical swarthy marauder who might have come from any of the countries east or west bordering on the Mediterranean. It was true he did have a nasty commercial smile. This, in Mado's experience, often denoted a second class talent, but if that were to be the worst of his faults, then there would not be too much to worry about.

'You know my name,' Mado said, 'what's yours?'

'Oh, I'll have a Scotch as well. Thank you, sir.'

Mado took the ancient riposte on the wing and nodded his head at the glass and bottle which the barman produced in one movement, as if by sleight of hand. Mado was fully alive to the fact that he himself was in some small way on trial. Each club of this kind has a different patron with individual ideas on how his own establishment should best be run.

Mado did not especially warm to this piratical-looking character, but he reminded himself that all such bosses had one invaluable common quality, without which they would not be in business at all: they knew who and what made the running in their own neck of the woods and they were always bang up to date. They were catalysts in the sense that they could, from time to time, affect events without in any way changing themselves. Clients might come and go, barmen at clubs such as the Al Fayoum went on for ever.

'Your very good health, sir. By the way my name is Sammy. Sammy the Wog.' The barman accompanied this with a sweeping glare as if daring Mado or anyone else to use the appellation at their peril. Mado, in turn, wondered what would happen if he did. A flash of the scimitar? A quick kick in the crutch?

'And how is 'o kyrios Marides,' the barman asked, allowing another indicator to fall into place, 'and his elegant wife? We hear he is very proud of his new son.'

'Is that the royal "we"?' Mado asked. Then, seeing a slight frown cross the barman's face, went on quickly, 'Both were in excellent fettle when I saw them last.'

'I was at one time a steward aboard his yacht – but that was long ago, before Mrs Tarnham arrived on the scene.'

'The *Myrmidia* used to be based on Piraeus,' Mado said.

'Yes, but before that the yacht belonged to a banker in Beirut – Monsieur Emile Duvinicole – as I expect you know. Well, it would be true to say Uncle Emile was more in shipping than in banks, but the two trades were almost interchangeable in Lebanon – in the old days, that is. And how did you find Beirut the other day?'

'You know so much about me,' Mado said, 'I'm sure you already know the answer to that one. Let me ask a question of you. What is the word on another Beiruti banker, Monsieur Bariolet?'

The barman smiled. You could cast him as Fagin, Mado thought in passing.

'I'm told the Phalangists are asking a high price for his release. You are interested in that? I'd have thought Mr Marides would prefer him where he is and out of the running. They used to be deadly rivals.'

'I don't suppose Panayotis cares very much either way,' Mado said, 'his attention is now elsewhere. However, if I did happen to be interested . . . ?'

The barman nodded.

'In Cairo that kind of information can be costly.'

'I don't know anywhere it isn't.'

'But as it is not your money . . . ?'

'So far as you or any other seller is concerned, it *is* my own money at stake.'

'And you justify every penny to your client?' The barman had a slight sneer in his voice.

'As a matter of fact I do, and always have,' Mado said sharply, 'though that has nothing whatever to do with you. And I'll thank you to keep it that way, Mr Sammy the Wog. To you I'm a principal.'

He noted the slight flinch at this sudden hardening of the banter. The battle lines were being drawn. Sammy dropped the sneer and paused, watching Mado carefully.

'Even if the price were half a million pounds?'

'Anything priced at half a million would have to be worth half a million.'

'And poor Monsieur Bariolet does not rate as highly as that? There are some who would say he is worth very much more.'

Mado laughed. This was some barman. Even Mr Zammit of the Santuario in Rome – a Sammy of another kind – did not talk as big as this.

'I'm not in the market for poor Monsieur Bariolet as you call him – or at any rate not yet.'

'Of coure not. You were a bystander, were you not? You were simply there when the snatch took place. Poor Ulf Achmed Aziz!'

'You are the second person tonight to commiserate on his death. Yes, I'm sorry, too, the old vulture got caught in the crossfire. He didn't deserve such an end.'

'However, Mr Mado, I am sure you did not come to the Club Al Fayoum to discuss Ulf Achmed Aziz. What *are* you in the market for, may I ask?'

'Nothing as yet.'

'Not even to meet Sheik Karim al Hammad?'

Mado stared at the barman with a keen dislike. There seemed to be nothing he did not know.

'No doubt the Sheik and I will be meeting without assistance from the market.'

'I wonder about that. The Sheik is a very elusive man.'

'That's one way of describing him,' Mado said. 'I have another.'

'Perhaps Madame Bariolet can help you. She and her husband know the Sheik well.'

'I realise that,' Mado said. And then, after a pause, 'She seemed to take her husband's abduction with remarkable fortitude – if you follow my meaning.'

'Oh I do, sir, I do. But then with the Bariolets of this

world, it is only a question of money, is it not? Money makes the world go round.'

It was obvious to Mado that Sammy the Wog was a highly informed man in a key position. It also struck him that Sammy would be unlikely to continue this friendly chitter-chat for long. Once he had sounded out Mado to discover how much he knew, or at least how many cards in his hand he would allow to be seen, then the climate would change.

'You asked me just now what I was in the market for,' Mado said as he fished out of his wallet a banknote of considerable size and watched it spirited away by Sammy without any suggestion that change might be forthcoming, 'what would you have on offer? Apart from a meeting with the Sheik?'

Sammy managed another nasty smile, and this time there could be no mistaking the message those crafty, twisted lips were conveying.

'I'll answer that question, sir, when you have something serious to ask.'

'If you're still around,' Mado said, pocketing his cigarettes and starting out for the door.

'Oh, *I* shall be around, sir, never fear about that. One or two others may not be, though.'

Now it was Mado's turn to manage a smile.

'A very pertinent observation,' he said as he reached the door. 'I'll be seeing you, Sammy, and thanks for the drink. I'm glad you're keeping ahead of inflation.'

'We do our best, sir. After all we were trained by the British.'

Even Marides would think ten pounds a drink a little high.

Mado had not been walking through the spice-scented Cairo night for more than five minutes before a large official-looking car cruised alongside, stopped and disgorged what Mado – from long experience – took to be the standard Mark II Gorilla Grab Squad. In a Moscow street they would have openly swaggered up to their victim as bystanders cowered away. In a city street of the supposedly free countries, the Gorillas made some slight pretence, ludicrous to an outside observer, of being ordinary law-abiding citizens only concerned to find out the time of day from their abductee.

As they came up to him, Mado turned towards them, put his hands somewhat jauntily on his hips and said in Russian,

'Don't bother with the frighteners. Look! I'm a volunteer. See? No shackles!'

Waving his hands in an abandoned way, he stepped into the back of the car and sat down next to his favourite Iron Curtain man, Colonel Ivan Karai.

'I'll bet that surprised you,' he said. 'Now you give *me* a treat – smile! And then tell me what the hell you think you're up to this time.'

'You have a great sense of humour, Mr Mado. That should stand you in good stead. General Simonov would like to have a talk with you.'

'You mean I'll be needing my sense of humour? I always find you Russians stretch it to the limit.'

The car set off at speed through the bustling night-life of Cairo of which he was no longer a part. It was a strange sensation. To be there and yet not to be there, sealed off and *en route* like some piece of food in a digestive tract which refuses to be broken down and absorbed. All round there was life, clatter, bustle and lights, and soon they would reach the Soviet Embassy from which no light ever shines. This trick of picking him up off a busy street had been played on Mado so many times before that now it had lost its former power to paralyse with fear.

As if he were reading his thoughts, Colonel Karai went on, 'You're not relying on your British passport, are you, Mr Mado?'

'For protection?' Mado said. 'Don't make me laugh. You think I'm that stupid? Rely on help from Whitehall? In

1976? However, Ivan,' he went on touching him gently on the knee as if making a gay pass, 'just you remember this. I do have friends elsewhere. Good, loyal, *effective* friends. You damage just one of these priceless grey hairs on my head, and I have friends who will make it their business to get you personally on to the slab and give you that lovely electric treatment around the testicles which you so enjoy giving to others. You doubt it? Don't worry, Ivan. Don't give it a thought. Rub me out and throw me on the dump. I know that's what you've long wanted to do – but before you do, hang on for a moment, dwell a pause, contain yourself in patience . . . because as sure as hell is to Brother Brezhnev, you'll be heading for the larkiest experience you'll ever have in your life.'

Mado turned towards the Russian and stared at him. Karai had a supercilious smile on his lips. It was like hammering a tank with a feather.

'You don't believe me, do you?' Mado said.

'I don't think it matters, Mr Mado.'

'That's what I thought,' Mado sighed. 'Ah well, there was a time when we'd have sent a gunboat. Now you uncivilised apes can behave here in Cairo just as you would in the streets of your own prison cities. What's up then? You imagine you control the world?'

'Of course, Mr Mado, I should have thought that must be obvious by now.'

The car sped on. Mado relapsed into silence and studied the Cairo scene as it passed by the windows of his little mobile prison. He felt slightly unwell.

5

If Mado felt queasy on his way to yet another assignation with the KGB, it was nothing to Andrea's feelings the next morning when she woke up in a strange bed stark naked and with some sort of cataleptic thunderstorm raging away in her head. 'Carambola!' she murmured, using for some reason she did not bother to fathom one of the more dated and arcane of her father's expletives. 'What happened to me?'

Since no one answered, she again opened her eyes and began to study her surroundings. The room and the bed were luxurious – when she had managed to hold them steady – and her clothes had been neatly folded and placed on a chair by an open door to a bathroom in which, she now realised, someone was taking a shower. For one absurd moment she wondered if it was George Mado up to another of his silly tricks, but a little later Micheline Bariolet appeared, resplendent in a lemon-coloured bathrobe and letting her hair down out of a shower cap.

'Ah, you're awake! *Comment ça va?* How do you feel?'

'Dreadful! What happened? Where am I? And how do I come to be here?'

'You passed out, darling, that's what happened. Don't you remember?'

'No,' Andrea said, 'I can't remember a thing.'

This was true. Her mind was in a haze, racing about in a loose crazy way as if she had literally been unhinged and had nothing to hold on to.

'Who slipped me the Micky Finn?' she asked and then added, 'Do you suppose I could have a couple of aspirins?'

'Of course,' Micheline said, 'they're there at the side of the bed – on my side of the bed.'

'Your side . . . ? God! have I spent the night in your bed?'

'It looks rather like it, darling,' Micheline replied with one of her sunniest smiles, 'but I don't know what would have happened if I'd let Pierre Labouchet get away with you last night.'

'And who's Pierre Labouchet when he's not trying to abduct me?'

'He's that Lebanese diplomat you fell for in such a big way.'

'What Lebanese diplomat? What are you talking about?'

'It may be a form of jet lag,' Micheline said, slipping into a pair of jeans and a bra-less top which seemed to show off her big beautiful nipples to perfection. 'It's happened to others, you know, Cairo's a longer journey from London than people think.'

'Somebody slipped me a very sophisticated drop of something last night. Was it you? And if so why?'

'Oh, come on!' Micheline said briskly. 'Why should anyone do a thing like that? Especially if you recall how you were trying to give it away last night. Frankly, darling, it was lucky you had me around.'

She paused and gave Andrea a sharp look.

'Now then, I have to go down to Alexandria this morning, so why don't you take a shower, clear that beautiful head of yours and come out on the terrace? There'll be some coffee and croissants for you in five minutes flat.'

Andrea sat up and then with a groan lay back again. A few seconds later she found the sheet whipped away and Micheline tugging at her hand.

'It's better to make an effort,' she said in a peremptory tone, as if suddenly becoming some sort of Commanding Officer. 'You don't want to stay here all day. You have a date with the

Syrian Ambassador, do you not? Let's see, in about an hour's time, isn't it? Take a shower. It will clear it all away.'

Now that she had been pulled out of bed and was somewhat unsteadily vertical, she realised that Micheline was only speaking common sense. Conscious of her late bedmate's reflective and slightly wanton smile at her nakedness, she tottered across to the bathroom, slid the door shut and turned on the shower. The events of the previous night were beginning to come back in a partial manner – but who was it who had given her the drug? What was it all about?

As soon as she had got herself together, had dressed and had become more or less herself again, she took a taxi back to the Hilton. The cassette of her interview with the President, together with her notes and address book, had been removed from her room, although nothing else appeared to have been disturbed.

Once through with the Syrian Ambassador, arrangements having been made for her trip to Damascus, Andrea sought out Lars Sweeney in the bar of the Hilton. He was engaged in what appeared to be intricate calculations concerning a race card, but lit up with pleasure at seeing her and abandoned the task.

'You stood me up again last night,' he said.

'I'm sorry about that, Lars . . .'

'Yes, well I'd just like to draw your attention to one of the more profound statements of our very own Mark Twain.'

'Lars, I'm in a rather fragile state.'

'Nothing, the great man said, needs reforming as much as other people's bad habits. Now you've fallen into the bad habit of standing me up. This kind of thing has got to stop.'

'Thanks.'

'That said, you look like a Bloody Mary could do you some good.'

'Thanks again. Provided you don't slip anything into it to improve its effect.'

She filled him in on all that happened – or rather on all she could remember of the events of the previous night, except for the bed bit. I wonder why I keep that to myself, she thought, he's no fool. But then no one ever tells the whole truth about sex. Only about other people's sex.

'Micheline seems to know a great deal about us and our friends,' Andrea went on. 'She wanted to know why you and George Mado were so interested in meeting Sheik Karim al Hammad.'

'And did you tell her?'

'How could I when I don't know myself?'

'Ah!' Sweeney said, looking away into the distance.

'But she reacted like a cat when I asked if she happened to be the "sleeper" in all this.'

Sweeney gave a short laugh and raised his eyebrows. He really was a good-looking man, Andrea thought, and felt a sudden urge to have him put his arms around her and hold her tight. How much better it would have been to have kept the date with him last night . . .

'That was some leading question! As a matter of fact, why *did* you ask her?'

'Instinct, I suppose.'

'Great! But what sort of answer did you expect? Hell, you don't ask the Pope about his sex life, do you?'

'I know one or two Fleet Street people who would.' She felt herself wilting slightly under the quizzical look those smoky grey eyes were giving her. They were good eyes, but she had no wish to face them now. 'Why are you so critical all of a sudden?'

'You're too attractive a woman,' Lars said, 'I could never hurt your feelings.'

'That I believe,' she said sarcastically.

'It happens to be true. I also happen to be very fond of you, Andy.'

'Yes, well, we won't go into that. You think I showed too much of my hand?'

'Honey, we all play poker in different ways. However it's always unwise to risk being caught on low threes.'

'You *have* hurt my feelings.'

'I don't think so,' Sweeney said, giving her a long, steady look. 'Throw in. Draw another hand.'

'Well . . .'

'Well what?'

'I don't suppose I'll be playing poker with you. What do you know about Micheline Bariolet that I don't know?'

'Now that's plain stupid. How could anyone answer a question like that?'

'You mean she *is* the Cairo Sleeper?'

'For God's sake, Andy! Yes, of course, one of them – sure! In every sense of the word.'

He paused for a moment, wondering how far he should take it. 'In any case, she repaid you in kind. She led you into a trap – you and all that Fleet Street sophistication.'

'At the cost of a cassette and a notebook. And there may be no connection in that.'

'You said your address book had gone.'

'Not the one that matters,' Andrea said. She was beginning to regret taking on Lars Sweeney in this particular way. 'Stupid I may have been with my direct question, but not *that* stupid.'

'Okay,' Lars said, as if talking to a child, 'then you're asking which side is she on? The goodies or the baddies?'

'Yes.'

'Perhaps both,' Lars said, getting her another drink, 'there's a lot of that about.'

'We know which side her husband is on.'

'I hope so. I wouldn't bet on it though.'

'And her son?'

'That creep, Pemberton Fuller? Incidentally, have you seen George Mado around this morning? He should have been in by now for his ration of malt whisky. The sun is over or under or sideways to the yardarm – or something damn silly like that.'

'Mado usually checks with me before getting on with the day's work. Preferably if I'm taking a shower.'

'And he didn't this morning?'

'Lars Sweeney, you *know* where I was this morning. I wasn't at the Hilton, was I? Why are you so worried? That Mado's always darting away on some lead or other. He'll show up.'

'He left in one hell of a hurry last night. Maybe Pemberton Fuller led *him* into some sort of trap . . .' Sweeney glanced away and then looked down at his race card. 'Oh well, there it is. I still have this problem about the 4.30 this afternoon.'

For a few moments both kept silent, engrossed in their own lines of thought.

'I suppose there's no doubt about General Sayyid, is there?' Andrea eventually said. 'And Micheline is a good friend of his.'

'There's doubt about any single main character in the Middle East,' Lars said. 'However, on present showing I'll grant you General Sayyid is a goodie and, yes, Micheline is one of his friends. In fact, a very good friend indeed.'

'Goodness gracious me! Great Scott and all that!' Andrea commented. 'Is there no one she doesn't go to bed with?'

'Does it matter? She has catholic tastes. After four millionaires, who wouldn't?'

Lars lit a cigarette.

'Micheline takes herself to be a latterday Cleopatra,' he went on after a pause, 'or Catherine the Great, if you like.

She's down in the record as someone who works and plays to excess. A high-voltage lady. Very dangerous to touch.'

'I know,' Andrea said a little ruefully. 'I seem to have shared her bed last night.'

'Lucky old you!' Lars said with an admiring smile. 'And I bet it cost you an effort to tell me.'

'Oh, you're all right! For an American. What do we do now?'

'Me – I think I'll check in with the office. See if they have anything on Mado.'

'Yes, but . . .'

'Yes but what?'

'Well, you may think this a bit silly but . . . It's not his firm, is it, Lars? The CIA I mean.'

Lars Sweeney looked at her as if he could scarcely believe his ears.

'That's right. It isn't, is it? However, my beautiful, gorgeous red-headed girl, do you not consider we still speak the same language? Especially in a city like Cairo?'

'You don't have to talk to me like a child, you know.'

'I don't know so much about that. I wonder what it was they slipped you last night. It seems to have affected this part of your anatomy,' he tapped his head, 'and you a newspaper woman.'

'Oh, come off it, Lars! We all know the CIA controls every city in the world. I just wondered whether they'd bother with someone like George Mado. After all he's only a small cog in what is now a cottage industry, isn't he?'

'Hey there – stop that chauvinism.'

'But it's true, isn't it? We don't count any more, do we?'

Sweeney decided to drop the banter. He stared at her with his grey-blue eyes and then launched out.

'Technically both George and I are independent and retired – for want of a better description. Neither of us connects directly any more. You know that perfectly well. I'm back in the law; George – well, I don't know what he would call himself if you asked him, an adviser or consultant of some kind, I suppose. Like who isn't these days? The point is a cat is a cat till he dies. The KGB, ourselves and British Security, whatever name it goes under, remain hopelessly enmeshed with each other, hopelessly intrigued with each other's personnel. I guess "intrigued" is a good all-purpose word, at the very least they're hopelessly involved in the day-to-day activities of the other two services. I'd say you're right, Andy' (later she remembered that this was the first conversation they'd had in which he'd called her by the affectionate diminutive she'd forgotten since her nursery days) 'in a sense we do run the world – the CIA and the KGB, I mean – or a fair share of it. So okay, I am going to check in with my folk about George Mado as I have done on occasion before. This time, though, I have a gut feeling of urgency. The stronger the Soviets become, the less attention they're forced to pay to the rules of the game, and the more they are apt to behave in Cairo as if they were only in Prague or Warsaw. Something's about to happen in this hot, smelly city . . .'

He paused for effect and then went on:

'If the timing looks in danger of going wrong, you know what they do? They sweep the board clean – remove any awkward pieces there may be around, that might get in the way.'

'You think what happened to me last night was connected with that?'

'Of course. Call it a warning shot across the bows, if you like. Or maybe they *did* find out what it really was they were after. The fact remains you'd just interviewed the President, you'd been specially asked to a Sayyid reception at short notice and you'd met Suleiman Masri. Then that gorgeous Micheline Bariolet, wife of the baddies' abducted paymaster, began a sudden unhealthy interest in you which may or may not have been concerned only with your glamorous physique. Are you receiving me loud and clear?'

She nodded unhappily. 'A little to much for comfort.'

'Well, then, over and out. When are you taking off for Damascus?'

'Tomorrow afternoon.'

'Right!' he said sharply, 'then see you later today, and this time make sure you're there. All of you and with this in working order.'

He tapped his head again and was about to go over to the bar to pay when Andrea reached over and took the chits out of his hand.

'I'll take care of these. Go and find out about Mado. I'm getting that urgent gut feeling too. And it's not gyppy tummy.'

In the safe house where he had been taken – he could not be sure if he was in a part of the embassy proper, since he had been subjected to the usual blindfolding process before being bullied out of the car with a maximum and unnecessary display of force – Mado at first thought they were holding him simply in order to keep him out of the way. But out of the way of what?

He had been thrown into an improvised prison cell and left to himself. The place stank of urine and the walls and door were alive with vermin. There were also traces of the standard brutality used on previous occupants. KGB methods did not change, whether in the Lubyanka or in some wretched cellar in Cairo. These were the nether regions on which international socialism relied for its power.

He thought about Anna and his children. He thought about Andrea and Micheline, about several long glasses of malt whisky and about some of the minor pleasures of freedom. It did him no good. It was all a monumental waste of time at this stage of his life. He lay down on the wooden bed and began counting the cockroaches on the ceiling. No doubt about it, he told himself, they've done it to you again, and at your age, sport, the fun wears thin. Depression began to set in, and as the hot night dragged on and on he wondered if perhaps, after all, this might be the way in which he would end his days.

The next morning they hauled him along to see General Simonov. The KGB chief was seated as always behind an oversize desk in which, no doubt, there would be every current listening and recording device which the Soviet bureaucracy considered essential for their purposes. Simonov and Mado knew each other of old, having first come up against one another in Operation Powder Train. Well, Mado thought as he studied the General some eight years later, at least Simonov was more of a human being than Ivan Karai. A small mercy, perhaps, but nevertheless one for which he was prepared to be grateful.

'I am sorry we had to give you an uncomfortable night,' Simonov said in Russian. Mado shrugged his shoulders and said nothing. He had long ago learnt the wisdom of letting the hostiles make the timing.

'It saves time,' General Simonov continued. 'Now, tell me what I need to know and we will then think about what to do next.'

'Tell you what? I'm getting a little old for this sort of thing. I work for Marides these days.'

'Still with the sense of humour,' the General observed drily and stared at him in silence.

'Suppose you tell me,' Mado said eventually. 'This time I really do *not* know what you're up to. Cairo has never been my scene.'

'Don't waste my time, Mr Mado.'

'Well, you're wasting mine. What do you want me to say?'

'Where is Henri Bariolet?'

'I don't believe it,' Mado said, a twisted smile round his

lips, 'I just don't believe it. You go to all the trouble of picking me up in a Cairo street to ask me something you already know and I don't? Incredible!'

'What did Pemberton Fuller offer to sell you yesterday?'

'May I say something, General? I think you're losing your grip. Henri Bariolet, Pemberton Fuller – you didn't get me here for this. So what is it you want?'

'It could be you, Mr Mado,' the General said with the trace of a smile in his eyes. With difficulty Mado suppressed the guffaw which he felt like giving.

'You must be joking,' he said in English. Then, to Mado's genuine surprise, the General reached down to a cupboard on the side of his desk and extracted a bottle of Scotch and two glasses. He further astonished Mado by dropping into comparatively colloquial English.

'Glenlivet says General Simonov is not.' He poured out two generous measures and passed one over to Mado.

'Never trust a Scot,' Mado said, raising his glass.

'We don't. We like their whisky, though.' The General raised his glass in an answering toast. 'You are right, Mr Mado. We did not get you here to find out what we already know. But now you are no longer in the British service, now that you accept a retainer of two thousand dollars a month from our friend, Panayotis Marides, it seemed to me that you might care to increase your earnings, without, of course, being in any way disloyal to your late employers, the British Government. That we would not be foolish enough to ask of any man with a distinguished career behind him.'

Mado wondered how they had found out the exact sum Marides was paying him. It went into his Swiss account and he did not think Pan would give away that sort of information. He studied the General warily over the rim of his glass. They must have someone working for them close to Panayotis Marides.

'I have no idea what you would want me to do,' he said, 'but

I must say you set about your recruiting in a very odd way. This,' and he raised his glass, 'is all very well. But why snatch me off the street and give me that disagreeable night among the cockroaches?'

General Simonov lit a long Russian cigarette and allowed another glint of a smile to creep into his eyes.

'My organisation does not like its employees to lose their respect. You understand what I mean?'

'Up the Establishment!' Mado said. Then, for good measure, 'Right up!'

He was still reeling somewhat from astonishment at this move. He sensed that anything could happen and the General's next remark proved this to be true.

'Up the Establishment!' General Simonov said.

'Come again?' Mado said. And then added quickly, 'I may have to lie down.'

'Of course. A shock is a shock. And just by chance you think all this is being recorded, you are at liberty to come round to this side of the desk and inspect the controls. As you know, our regulations require them always to be placed in the second drawer down on the left. Here, see for yourself.'

He beckoned Mado round, pulled open the drawer in question, which contained the standard switch gear for the recording circuits and which, to Mado's increasing surprise, were all in the 'off' position. Looking down at the drawer, he realised how easy it would be to grapple the General from above.

As if reading his thoughts, General Simonov said, 'Does that prove my good faith? Here I am for the moment at a disadvantage. Now please go back to your side of the desk.'

'Are there not strict instructions . . . ?' Mado began, but did as he was told.

'That recordings are always to be made of any "private" interview of this kind? Naturally. You have a working knowledge of our regulations as we have of yours. And in a moment or so I shall switch on the machine and repeat something of what I have just asked you. This was, as I said, to prove my good faith.'

It suddenly flashed through Mado's mind that the General's real objective might not be to suborn him to the Russian service but possibly to lay the route open for the opposite to happen. Could it be that General Simonov was thinking of defecting to the West? It was unlikely, but stranger things than that had already happened in thirty years of Cold War.

'Before you switch on the fruit machines, will you level with me, General?'

Simonov gave him a sharp flash of the eyes.

'If I can. But you will have to be quick.'

'What is your current operation aimed at?'

'The removal of a very important person who stands in our way.'

'And the timing?'

'Immediate.'

The General nodded curtly, reached down to the second drawer on the left and, Mado presumed, switched on the tape recorders. When he next spoke, it was in the firm tones of Dzerzhinsky Square.

'You may sit down, Mr Mado. You are here of your own free will. You are here because you have expressed a wish to help Socialism. Good. Now, tell us what we require to know and we need not keep you more than a few minutes. Is that understood?'

Without giving Mado a chance to reply, the General again nodded and went on, 'First of all, who arranged the abduction of the banker Bariolet?'

'Well,' said Mado, deciding to go along with this charade in its early stages, 'I can't really be sure but I imagine it must have been that Lebanese club owner, Ulf Achmed Aziz.'

'You were actively concerned in the operation?'

'No. I was there at the time – accidentally, as it happens – simply because I was trying to contact Monsieur Bariolet.'

'On behalf of your Whitehall masters.'

'If you say so.'

'I do not say anything of the kind. I am asking you.'

'Gawd!' said Mado. 'How absurd can you get? No, not on behalf of Whitehall. I am now a consultant employed by Panayotis Marides.'

'You are still a paid lackey of Whitehall.'

'I tell you, I am no longer in British Government service.'

'You are lying, Mr Mado. Don't waste my time.'

'Have it your way, sport. It's your matinée.'

'You are on Russian soil, Mr Mado. You do not speak to a Russian General in a frivolous manner.'

It was interesting, Mado reflected afterwards, that Simonov used the word 'Russian' instead of 'Soviet'. Interesting, perhaps, but not significant.

'Look, General. You and I know each other of old. Why don't we just get down to brass tacks? We may be technically on Russian soil. We are still here in Cairo and not in Moscow. Cairo, General, Cairo.'

At that moment a subordinate gorilla slipped into the room in a nervous way. This did not please General Simonov who glared at the intruder.

'I did not ring,' he said in Russian, 'why did you interrupt?'

'Excuse me, sir, but there is an American here to see you.'

'An American? I have no appointment with any American.'

'He says you will see him.'

The General gave vent to a Russian oath. 'Does he, indeed? Tell Colonel Karai to deal with him.'

'Colonel Karai is not in the embassy.'

The General pressed a button on his desk intercom. There was no reply.

'Where is Colonel Karai?'

'I don't know, sir. He had an appointment at the Ministry but he has not returned.'

The General picked up the phone, hesitated for a second or two and then put it back. 'The American will wait.'

There was the noise of a scuffle outside the door, which suddenly burst open. Lars Sweeney strode in followed by two of the embassy staff who were trying somewhat uncertainly to restrain him.

'What is the meaning of this?' General Simonov asked furiously.

'He says "Diplomat", sir.'

The KGB still hesitate to use physical force on diplomats abroad. In the Soviet Union itself this nicety does not apply. But in the West, where they are open to the charge of not being 'cultured', and in the Third World, there is still a Soviet diffidence in laying hands on a foreign emissary.

'I'm not diplomatische, as it happens,' Lars said, striding up to the desk and paying no attention to Mado, 'but it got me in.'

'Arrest this man,' Simonov said in Russian and the two staff men leapt forward.

'George!' Lars said as he swung a nicely placed punch, winding one of the Gorillas. Moving fast, as he could do so well, Mado sprang out of his chair and had the other by the arm in a quick screw which made the victim cry out in pain. General Simonov pressed the alarm button, and in a trice the room seemed to fill up with huge turnip-headed men who quickly freed their comrades and held both Lars and Mado in vice-like grips.

'Washington is going to hear about this,' General Simonov growled. He was very angry indeed and there was no doubt about that.

'I don't think so, General,' Lars said, 'or you won't see Karai again.'

This had a stunning effect on Simonov who signed to the

gorillas to release their charges. A short silence followed.

'Why not ask the audience to leave?' Lars went on with a pleasant smile. 'That way we can talk.'

For a second or two Mado thought Simonov would explode. Then with supreme self control, Simonov ordered the guards to leave the room. Mado caught Simonov's eye and gestured to him to turn off the recording apparatus, and again, after a moment's thought, he did so.

'That's better,' Mado said and, turning to Lars, proffered his hand.

'Dr Livingstone, I presume.'

'Now,' said General Simonov, 'you had better talk and talk with speed.'

'Easy!' Lars said. 'You had Mado: we now have your nice Colonel Karai.'

'Incredible!' General Simonov murmured in a low voice. 'You don't seriously think you're going to get away with this? This is provocation to an absurd degree.'

'Sure it's provocation. But the fact remains – you'll never see him again. He'll just disappear. He should never have been in that male brothel anyway.'

'What are you talking about?' Simonov exclaimed in a rising tide of anger. 'Colonel Karai does not frequent establishments of that kind.'

'But that is where his body will be found. Or it might be at the bottom of the Red Sea in a nice weighted sack. Whichever you prefer. And I have news for you about Colonel Karai's sexual tastes.'

'My Ambassador shall take care of this instantly and at once.'

'I don't think so, General. I don't think your Ambassador is even going to hear of it. This is between you and me. After all, this is exactly what the KGB does in every non-Communist city, where you brag you can get away with it. You make a snatch, cry provocation and hide behind your diplomatic immunity. Great, if you get in first. However, you Russians don't seem to be very popular in Cairo these days. It's not your scene any more. And people so easily disappear. I tell you, General, Karai will never be found. You know and I know that he's not officially in the country – and something tells me that you need him around for the operation you're about to launch. Well, we needn't go into that, but that's the weak spot in your armour, General. We all know Karai could never come in through the front door anyway – ever. We also appreciate how slowly and obstructively Egyptian bureaucrats work when they're minded that way. Well, General, in this case the whole damned thing is going to be so slow, you're not going to detect a single sign of life.'

He smiled in an easy way at the KGB General, who had resumed his seat and was staring fixedly at an ashtray on his desk.

'Poor Colonel Karai!' Lars Sweeney went on. 'He was such a great little guy. And I'd heard it rumoured that *Russian Playboy* was going to make him Gulag Playmate of the month. Tch tch tch! Too bad!'

He paused for effect and then added in a sharper tone of voice, 'Now pick up that phone and tell your muscle men to let us out the front door. George, are you okay?'

Mado returned him a mock salute and together they made their way to the door as Simonov picked up the phone.

Once they were out in the street, Mado said, 'Well, thank you, Lars, Nelson had nothing on you when it comes to a cutting-out operation. How did you grab Karai?'

'I didn't,' Sweeney said with a private smile, 'I just organised a little delay. I got our boys to ambush the Colonel and let Cairo traffic do the rest. I said to give me an hour, and they did. But now we'll have to work fast. The President's gone.'

'Gone?'

'Gone. Disappeared. Been hijacked. Abducted. Call it what you like – he's not there any more.'

'How?'

'I don't exactly know how. And it doesn't matter, not right now. The point is – there's no Head of State here in Cairo. Not at the moment.'

Mado thought this out for a moment or so. 'Then who takes over?'

'The Vice-President, I suppose. Actually, General Sayyid will be the man who matters. Unless they have him as well.'

'And who's they?'

'Your guess is as good as mine. The Libyans? The Israelis? I doubt the Israelis. Cairo isn't Entebbe. It may simply be a Palace revolution.'

'Major Suleiman Masri?'

'That could be nearer the mark. And certainly our friends – the ones we've just left – will be in it. On that you can rely one hundred per cent. That's why Simonov let us go – he couldn't risk Karai being removed from the scene at a critical time.'

'Ah yes,' Mado said, 'this begins to make sense. And that leads us back once more to our old friend Tarnham – the Sheik Karim al Hammad. Let's get ourselves a drink.'

'Do you never think of anything else?' Lars said, and then relaxed. 'Well, okay, it's a great idea.'

6

The operation, and its cover plan, had evidently been very well prepared. The media gleaned little immediately beyond the bare facts that an attempted abduction had taken place and that a State of Emergency had been proclaimed together with a complete news blackout. All frontiers were simultaneously closed. Cairo Radio announced first that an attempted kidnap of the President had failed. No details were given in the interests of security but, the announcement claimed, the President was alive and well and later on would address the nation on the radio. The television service went off the air due, it was said, to a number of technical faults.

The government directed that business and private life should continue as normal, except that during the Emergency martial law would prevail and until the matter had been investigated a curfew would be imposed. The military were in evidence and so were tanks in strategic positions, but all troops not required for policing the populace had been confined to their barracks. In fact inevitable chaos had begun.

'The story I get is this,' Lars said after he and Mado had checked with their respective Embassies. 'The President's plane landed or was forced to land, no one seems to be sure, at an improvised desert airstrip somewhere to the west of Asyut, where the President was going to inspect a new irrigation project. There the personal staff were overpowered by commandoes in foreign uniform – Israeli, Libyan, again no one knows for sure – and the President was taken away in a helicopter, and probably transferred yet again to a low flying plane which could dodge the radar screen – so he's likely to be either in Israel or in Libya. Both countries deny that he is, but then they would, wouldn't they?'

'I thought the announcement said the kidnap attempt had failed?'

'That's right. The early announcements did. The only discrepancy in it all is that the President and those members of the government who matter don't seem to be around any more.'

'Ah!' said Mado, taking a swig at his drink.

'Look, George, at this time of deep international crisis, don't you think you could manage some kind of comment a little more profound than just "Ah!"?'

'Ah!' said Mado deliberately. 'Now here's another theory. Suppose the whole thing is a put-up job? Suppose it suited the President to disappear – to make it seem as if he'd been hijacked – so as to entice the real plotters to come out into the open?'

Lars pondered this for a while. All round them the Hilton bar buzzed, no doubt, with similar speculation.

'Kind of an extreme measure to take, don't you think? He's not another Papa Doc, is he? Egypt is no banana republic.'

'You just prised me out of the Russian Embassy by means of a dastardly trick. Suppose the President or someone near him wanted to work the same idea?'

'But why?'

'Because there *is* a plot: abduction and/or assassination. We know that. Probably the latter – except that assassination is a little too final if the hostile element were to have some sort of deal in view.'

'For Christ's sake,' Sweeney said tetchily, 'you and Dr Kissinger. *What* kind of deal? This is the President of a country, a key country in the Middle East. Come on, George, quit horsing around. What "deal" could possibly merit the setting up of this degree of crisis or pseudo-crisis?'

Now it was Mado's turn to keep silent. Both were watchful and wary, both especially alert for the sudden appearance in the bar of enemies or friends. In times of crisis, the bar of a hotel such as the Cairo Hilton fills with a clientele not usually seen in such surroundings. To Mado's sharp eyes it seemed as good a place as any for a discussion of this kind, so he did not at once react to his colleague's irritated questioning; he realised only too well that it disguised a deep uncertainty which he shared.

Mado looked across the room wishing fervently that he were several thousand miles away in his suburban living room about to read his elder daughter a bedtime story, instead of being nastily involved in a fairy tale of a different sort. He tried to marshal the facts in his mind. What deal, indeed, could possibly be worth the attention of Paul Tarnham, the whole weight of the KGB and involve the disappearance, intentional or otherwise, of the Egyptian President?

'I think the Naval Attaché may well be right,' Mado said in the end.

'What's the Naval Attaché got to do with it?'

'The Naval Attaché here is an old friend of mine,' Mado said, still looking into the distance, 'and I had a word with him just now when I was in the embassy. There are two Russian aircraft carriers in the Red Sea to the south of the Suez Canal and two more in the Mediterranean off Alexandria. There are other Soviet capital units based on Tripoli in Libya, with support forces in Benghazi. Somalia is theirs. Just suppose for a moment that this "deal" we're on about concerned the taking over – or rather the recapture – of Egypt for the Soviet Imperialists, or at the very least the bringing back of Egypt into the Soviet sphere of influence, Suez Canal and all. You don't think that might justify the stakes?'

'And how about World War Three?'

'I don't think the seizing of Egypt would start that one off.

Not enough real incentive in it for either side. But there's no doubt it would be a bloody good exercise. It would also show how far the US and Soviet Russia were prepared to go before calling it a day. A sort of latterday Cuba and the missiles if you like.'

'You really think they might risk it?' Lars asked, and suddenly the difference in their ages and their two life experiences hit Mado as if he had accidentally banged down on his funny bone. He studied the American's firm jaw, the intelligent eyes and the 'film star' good looks with which Lars Sweeney had been endowed by his Swedish mother and his Irish-American father.

'You've done stints in Russia and other Eastern bloc countries many a time, haven't you, Lars?'

The American nodded.

'And yet you ask if they could do it! After Czechoslovakia there's no possible way of holding them back. They're perpetually high on Force. Military might – that's all they believe in. You know, I know, and they most certainly know, they can get away with it.'

Mado clenched his fist and stuck it in Lars' face.

'That's their culture, and you know it. Individual intimidation on one level: tanks and attack carriers on another.'

'Oh sure,' Lars said, 'you speak from experience.' There were times when he thought Mado tedious and boring, although he was forced to respect the strong feelings which animated the man when he talked like this.

'I do.' Mado said soberly. 'The Lubyanka takes care of any illusions about human nature you may happen to cherish. I've also just had a nasty night in one of their local foyers of culture. I *know* what those apes can do. The point is will they do it? Will they actually take the risk? Both our services know they could seize Egypt in forty-eight hours once the word is given.' He snapped his fingers. 'They could do it like that – and by the time the West wakes up, if it ever does, it's all going to be a little too late. Huh! try to force Ivan out of Czechoslovakia now,' he laughed bitterly, 'never! They're there and there they're going to stay. It could be the same here in Egypt. If the Israelis can do Entebbe, the Russians can do the Delta. All that is holding them back is the price they might have to pay. So if Sadat *could* be got out of the way, if that boy scout from Libya can do their dirty work for them – and after all, he's had enough practice in Ulster, Uganda and the Lebanon – then they *might* even get the job done without risking a single airborne division. Egypt could drop into their lap much as Somalia and Libya did. No bloodshed and a rich picking for those in the know.'

'There's a slight difference in size between Egypt and Libya. Like nearly twenty to one in numbers.'

'There's also a slight difference in fighting quality too. Ask any old Turk – or a young Israeli.'

'The October war? All those Heroes of the Crossing?'

'That myth isn't going to last them for ever. It's wearing out daily in the fleshpots of Cairo, as it always has done before. The Egyptians are just not a military nation.'

'Which brings us back to Suleiman Masri,' Lars remarked. 'I wonder what the brave Major is up to today.'

Mado put down his glass and stood up.

'I think I'll go and buy myself another ten-pound drink from Sammy the Wog. He said he'd answer any question when I had something serious to ask.'

'You devil, you,' Lars said. 'That leaves me with the much harder task of checking up on Andrea Eckersley. Don't let them take you in again, George. I can't pull that trick a second time.'

'No,' Mado said as he began moving away from the bar, and then stopped. 'Although it might be nice if we did actually remove Karai and that dear General Simonov from the scene, like you made out you did when you rescued me.'

'It's a great idea, George. I can visualise the reaction from Washington.'

'I'll just leave you with this thought for the day,' Mado said. 'I have a feeling that my old friend, General Simonov, might conceivably like to be abducted out of it all. It could be he's had enough.' He nodded a farewell to Sweeney.

'As a matter of fact I know how he feels.'

Mado, indeed, had come much nearer the mark than he had any means of knowing. In the Russian Embassy a first-class row had blown up over the timing of the coup then taking place. That afternoon 'the Sheik' had arrived back from Libya. He had been forced to travel via Rome since direct communications between Egypt and her neighbour to the west had been cut, and indeed the aircraft in which Tarnham travelled was the last to be allowed to land at Cairo Airport. When he reached the embassy he at once sent for General Simonov.

'Who gave the orders?' he demanded with an angry scowl. Simonov did not answer. 'I presume you did, General.'

'No.'

'Are you telling me the operation started itself?'

'The operation for which I am responsible has not begun.'

'What the hell do you mean?' When Tarnham was in a rage, he lapsed back into English and the upper-class accent he had acquired as a boy. 'The snatch took place this morning.'

'Exactly. Ours was planned for tonight in Aswan.'

'Then who jumped the gun? And who allowed it to happen?'

Simonov shrugged his shoulders. 'Masri has gone ahead without our authority. He was always headstrong, difficult to control.'

'Spare me the character analysis. Someone has made a fool

of us. Who is it? Major Masri? Someone has taken our careful plan and applied it a day early. How can that have happened?'

'The Sheik may be better able to answer that question than I,' Simonov said coldly. 'I did not negotiate with Masri's unit. You did. The Sheik cannot put the blame on me for that.'

'That,' Tarnham said ominously, 'will be discussed elsewhere and by others.'

'Of course it is possible,' Simonov suggested in a casual tone of voice, 'that our liaison with the New Revolutionary Committee was at fault. That, of course, is Colonel Karai's affair.'

'Leave Karai out of this. The operation is under your command.'

'Certainly, and Karai is directly under my orders. I'm merely telling you what I think may have happened. I can take care of the disciplinary side.'

'Where is the President?'

'At this moment in the safe place we planned.'

This was untrue. Simonov had no idea of the whereabouts of the President. However he had had enough experience of crucial situations never to admit to ignorance or doubt until – to use one of this hated English defector's phrases – he had been properly 'bowled out'.

There was a knock at the door and Karai entered the room. He wore a smirk of satisfaction and without being given permission to speak, said, 'The announcement has been made. The New Revolutionary Committee has seized authority. Communications and the broadcasting network have been taken over. The President is deposed. Major Masri claims to have the full support of the armed forces.'

'What is the real situation?' Simonov cut in.

'Unclear. There is fighting in the naval barracks at Alexandria. Army units south of Helwan have yet to declare.'

'In other words, Masri has Cairo and that's about all?'

'He has the Delta,' Karai said, 'Port Said and Suez are ours.'

The telephone rang on General Simonov's desk.

'Yes,' said Simonov, looking at Tarnham, 'the Sheik is with me now . . . I'll tell him.' He put down the phone and continued to Tarnham, 'Major Masri would like to see you at once. He's sending a car.'

'I'll take an embassy car.'

Simonov gazed at him calmly and coldly.

'I am in command of operations here in Egypt. The Sheik will take the transport sent by Major Masri. In that way he will be certain to arrive at his destination.'

Mado did not go to the Club Al Fayoum. After leaving the Hilton it had been his intention to walk to the Club, and indeed he had already started on his way when he suddenly became aware of being trailed. Dodging quickly into a doorway he watched the car stop, and then to his relief saw that it was driven by his friend – or it could be his enemy – of the previous night. Abdul, the taxi-driver who spoke Russian and who worked for the Egyptian Ministry of State Security. He walked across and got into the car.

'The effendi has sharp eyes in the back of his head.'

'Were you sent to keep me under surveillance?'

'I thought the effendi might need a taxi.'

'An excellent thought,' Mado said, giving him a long steady look, and then after a pause: 'Did you know where I was going?'

'I could make a guess. But I think the effendi will find Club Al Fayoum not open today.'

'Ah!' Mado again made his favourite noise which had so irritated Lars Sweeney, 'a wise precaution, no doubt, in view of the news.'

'Where would the Pasha like to be driven?'

'Surbiton, Surrey. But you'll have to take some extra petrol aboard.'

Abdul smiled.

'I, too, have a family,' he said, 'and like the effendi I have seen very little of them these last few days.'

'Let's work this out now,' Mado said. 'We could go to the Pyramids. Presidents may come and Presidents may go but tourism goes on for ever.'

'That is good thinking, sir. Touristic hotels with full modern equipment also go on through a crisis.'

'And the nice girls who frequent them.'

'That, too, sir.'

'It's a bright idea, Abdul, but my mind isn't quite on it today.' He gave the Egyptian another long, steady look. 'Do you know what happened to me when I left the Club Al Fayoum last night?' The driver did not answer except for the trace of a nod. 'Perhaps your touristic hotel is a similar trap.'

'Last night was last night and orders once given must be obeyed. But today is another day.'

'Ah!' said Mado. 'I'm not going to argue with the Koran. What are you trying to tell me, Abdul?'

'The effendi was interested in Pemberton Fuller, late of the CIA.'

'Yes.'

'He was taken away last night and shot.'

They stared at each other in silence for a moment or so.

'Poor bastard!' Mado said and prolonged the pause. 'Not that I really took to him as a friend. Do you know why he was shot?'

'He was a double agent. He made too many mistakes.'

'And what about you, Abdul?'

'I am for Egypt, effendi. So I am for the winning side. Perhaps I am a triple or four-time agent. Who can tell? In time everything will be rewarded.'

'A good statement,' Mado remarked, 'but in view of Major Masri's coup, which is the winning side now?'

'Nothing is certain, sir. I am only a taxi-driver.'

'Very well, Abdul. You are only a taxi-driver – but you seem to be very interested in me.'

'I have been told to take care of you.'

'*Take care* of me? What does that mean? Did you take care of me last night?'

'It was effendi's own decision to go to Club Al Fayoum. We met last night by accident.'

'But when you found out who I was and where I wanted to go . . .'

'Naturally I had to make my report. Today, though, is another day.'

'Perhaps I'm more stupid even than I look,' Mado said grittily, 'but don't you have orders for today?'

'Only to take care of the Pasha.'

'And lead me into another trap.'

'That would not be to take care of my client, would it?'

'I don't know,' Mado said, feeling suddenly tired, 'it depends on who is giving you the orders, on whether this coup is going to succeed, on what constitutes a trap.'

'Exactly, sir. We share the same predicament.'

'Hey! that's a big word!'

'But remember, sir, when this is over I shall still be driving taxi in Cairo, you will be back to England – if we survive, that is.'

For a brief moment Mado saw clearly how it was to be someone like Abdul living in a country such as Egypt, subjugated for so long by the Turks and then by the British and now once more the prize which Russian imperialism had set itself to win.

As if reading his thoughts, Abdul said, 'If only they would all leave us alone. Egypt can look after herself, but only if you leave us alone – you, the CIA and the KGB. We are not to be bought and sold any more. We simply want to live our own lives and be free. Even with Israel we can make a deal, but not with America shouting one thing and Gaddafi and the Russians another . . .'

'What is behind Major Masri's coup?'

'I do not understand.'

'Is it Russian of American money?'

'I am only a taxi-driver . . .'

'Yes, yes, yes. Or is it just that Masri wants power for himself?'

'Major Masri is a Hero of the Crossing. So, too, is our President – *the* Hero of the Crossing.'

'So why should one want to take power from the other?'

And then Abdul said something which electrified Mado because it confirmed an instinctive idea he had put earlier to Sweeney.

'Perhaps he doesn't. Perhaps both want to bring out into the open the real enemies of Egypt. See it this way, effendi. We Egyptians are idealists. But alas, we have a long history of corruption behind us. Perhaps the President wants to discover who has been bought – and by whom.'

'This could be the start of a lovely friendship,' Mado said. 'Why don't you drive me to your modernistic hotel and I'll buy you a drink?'

'Aywah, effendi,' Abdul said, and put the ancient Chevrolet into gear.

As soon as Mado had left the Hilton bar, Lars Sweeney contrived to pinpoint to his reasonable satisfaction the two men in the room who, he thought, were watching him and then deliberately and slowly left the bar himself. Once out of the hotel it took him about ten minutes and three changes of taxi to shake off his surveillance, and he then made his way to the safe house near the Bab el Luq métro station which was the CIA operational headquarters at that particular time. There he learnt of the murder of Pemberton Fuller, and also of the fact that whatever it was Pemberton Fuller had had to sell, he had not succeeded in passing it across.

'Who killed him?' Sweeney asked the operational chief of staff.

'Khaliq's men. The PITO adjustment squad. His girl-friend Ephrosini set it up shortly after she'd taken him to Masri's house.'

'Do we know where the President is?'

The Chief of Staff shook his head glumly. 'Nor can we get in touch with General Sayyid. Masri, at the moment, has it all under control. Or it looks that way.'

'Has anyone checked on Madame Bariolet?'

'Not since last night when she put a fast one over on Andrea Eckersley.'

'Who has the cassette and the notebooks?'

'We have them. As soon as we saw what was happening to the lady, we thought we'd better secure what material she had before it fell into other hands. We were just in time. Half an hour later, a couple of PITO men searched her room at the Hilton but they left it as clean as we did – so it looks like they were after the same material.'

'Was there anything of value in the cassette?'

'No. It was a straight interview with the President – the usual profile questions and answers.'

'So why the interest in the girl anyway?'

'She met Tarnham in London – as the Sheik, of course. Maybe they plan to use her in some way.'

'She pretends not to know the Sheik's real identity.'

'She knows all right. We asked London to fill her in before she left for Cairo.'

'Why?'

'We're not sure we can rely on your friend Mado.'

'Not rely on *Mado*? Oh come on!'

'Take it easy, Lars. In one respect only, is what I was going to add. He has such an emotional hang-up about Tarnham. We're not sure what he might do.'

'Come *on*, Harry! George Mado is no killer. In any case he's not on the active list.'

'He has killed in his time.'

'Only in self-defence.'

'Yes, well, the computer says he might do so again. And the last thing we want is Tarnham dead. In the previous three years the most dangerous, or the riskiest, move Dzerzhinsky Square has made – from their point of view that is – was to let that guy loose again in the Middle East. He's been leading us to people we never knew existed before. He's invaluable, Lars. Just so he goes on, that's all I ask. We want no hot head like Mado taking a crack at him out of anger, revenge or any other motive. The computer . . .'

'Screw the computer!' Lars said with unusual force. 'Has Micheline Bariolet yet been told about her son's murder?'

'We don't know.'

'How's that?'

'For the simple reason we don't know where she is. She was supposed to go to her Alexandria house this morning, but she never showed up.'

'Why not ask the computer that?' Lars said, preparing to leave. 'I'll get her for you. Do you want her brought in?'

'Certainly not. Find her, yes. Talk to her, yes. But like Tarnham she's of much more value when she's out and around.'

'My guess is she's in bed with Sayyid. She has something of an Olympic track record for the bed.'

Once the news about the President's disappearance had broken, Andrea tried to see General Sayyid. She found his residence closely guarded. No one was to be allowed in past the gate, and when she tried to get round this obstruction she found herself promptly under arrest. Indeed, had it not been for her press credentials, she would have been kept restricted at the pleasure of the New Regime.

As it was, the young captain who was locally in charge (latterday revolutionaries never seemed to rank much above captain, it seemed to Andrea, and no doubt the next wave would improve downwards to corporals and sergeants) only agreed reluctantly to release her on being assured that she would return forthwith and directly to the Hilton hotel.

In fact this suited her very well. She had originally intended not to write her profiles whilst on circuit, so to speak, but to complete them all after returning to England. Now, in view of the coup and its aftermath, she went to her room in the Hilton and at once began pounding out her piece on the first of her chosen subjects – the President, who could scarcely be more in the news than he was at that very moment.

She had been working for about an hour when she heard a knock at the door and, as she went to open it, the telephone rang. It was Lars Sweeney at the door and General Sayyid's ADC on the phone.

Waving to Lars to sit down, she said into the phone, 'You're right, I *have* just tried to see General Sayyid . . . well, of course it's about the coup – the abduction – the news . . . yes . . . ah! he *will* see me now? Right. And you'll send a car just like last night. Thank you. I'll be waiting outside on the steps.'

She put down the phone and looked at Lars.

'Well, now, how about that? The General is prepared to talk to me after all.'

'Who says it's the General? Was that Sayyid himself?'

'No. I think it was the ADC who rang last night.'

They looked at each other for a moment or so in silence, which Andrea broke by saying, 'And what can I be doing for you, Lars Sweeney?'

'You could have dinner with me tonight. No, hold it. That was the idea for yesterday, wasn't it?'

'It'll stay good enough for today as well. Except that every time we make a date we seem to provoke some new disaster.'

'Next question. How do I contact your sexy friend, Micheline Bariolet?'

'Your guess is as good as mine. She told me she was going to Alexandria this morning.'

'She never made it.'

'Maybe she changed her mind.'

'It could be she found out about her son.'

'Pemberton Fuller? What about Pemberton Fuller?'

Lars filled her in on that piece of news.

'And it looks like another notch on the tally of your ex-Oxford graduate, Mustapha Khaliq. He and his hench lady, Ephrosini, took care of the hit. It's getting to be like it was in Rome when something diabolical seemed to be planned for that next Saturday in Milan. Only this time the pace gets quicker.' He lit a cigarette and looked at her through the smoke. 'You know something? You're too goddam attractive by half. I rarely come up with a statement of this kind. So stop turning me on.'

'Oh! you'll get over it,' Andrea said, but in spite of herself an old-fashioned blush came to her cheeks, 'just keep your mind on the job. You know what's been worrying me? It's the way Micheline Bariolet was aware of all I was up to and when, who I was going to see, my trip to Damascus, etcetera etcetera.'

'Plus the fact she now knows you more personally than I do myself.'

Andrea seemed to withdraw like a tortoise pulling its head back under its shell. Then she stared at him in as cold a way as she could contrive.

'If you want to advance your suit with me, Lars Sweeney, you'll have to give up making remarks of that kind. Just try being a gentleman for five straight minutes and see how you get on.'

'Are you going to see Sayyid?'

'Of course.'

'Would you like me to come along?'

'Thank you, Sir Galahad. As a matter of fact, I would. Unfortunately, though, I don't think General Sayyid would appreciate the gesture.'

'Well . . . take care of yourself.'

She went over and kissed him gently, noting with private amusement the slight shock of surprise he evinced at her kissing him of her own volition.

'It's sweet of you to mind. I didn't know lawyers could be so nice.'

'Lawyers in the plural are not,' Lars said shortly, 'only this singular American one – the crazy fool.'

He pulled her back to him and gave her another long lingering kiss. 'And don't forget you have a dinner date to-night, which this time you're going to make.'

'I hope so,' Andrea said, mentally touching wood.

7

As 'the Sheik' drove to Revolutionary HQ in the armoured car which had been sent for him, he pondered on several of the unsatisfactory aspects of the current operation. He felt irritated, sharp and ill-at-ease. In the first place, since Moscow had initiated, developed and paid for the situation which had now come about, it should more properly have been Major Masri driving to see him than the other way round. Moscow had always been cautious and doubtful about Masri. Like the peasant from next-door Libya, the Russians appreciated that he had fire and charisma, intensity of purpose and courage – all of which it was expedient to harness to the Soviet purpose.

But the young Major had also shown himself to be dangerously independent. His valour, guts and success in the October war had, in Tarnham's opinion, gone to his head. Very early on, Moscow had decreed him to be of use only for a limited period. Thereafter he would become a liability. There was nothing new in that: if the CIA used computers, then Moscow had sixty years' direct practical experience in the promoting of revolution and in its *post facto* control. Masri's character had been considered in depth before any suppport at all for the mini-revolution had been given.

The highly secret second and third phases of the operation, about which, of course, Masri had not been informed, would entail the Major's inevitable removal from the seat of power. Nothing new about that. After all, Nasser had removed Neguib almost as soon as he had got rid of King Farouk.

But whilst still in the saddle, there remained one paramount decision Masri and Masri alone must be compelled to take, and one which in the planning stages he had reluctantly promised only after the greatest display of obtuseness and dissimulation. This key requirement would be to invite units of the Russian fleet to visit Egyptian ports 'as a security precaution'. This had had to be agreed before money and supplies were forthcoming from Soviet sources, but, as Tarnham knew only to well, it was an accord made under duress and one which the Egyptians would avoid carrying out if they possibly could. The Russians were not popular in Egypt, and least liked of all, perhaps, was the Russian fleet. The invitation to return, therefore, had not been lightly promised.

'We do not want the hand of friendship as you gave it to Prague in 1968,' Masri had said.

'Ships are not tanks,' Moscow had replied, giving him the soft soap. 'The revolution will be yours and in no circumstances whatever will Russian naval guns fire upon Egyptian targets. You will be granted such military support as you need and this support will be at your sole discretion – that is the hand of friendship from us to you. The Navy is something else. On our part we require the renewed use of Egyptian ports as we had them in the great Nasser days. That is all we are asking – and that will be the hand of friendship from you to us.'

Many hands had then been dutifully shaken, but Tarnham remained unconvinced that this definitive promise would be kept. Hence, now, he was showing himself only too ready to waive protocol as to who should go to see whom. He would wait on Major Masri and he would stay on target, however much face he might be losing in the opinion of the Moscow bureaucrats. He would not leave Masri until the necessary invitation and the enabling orders had duly been authorised.

Sheik Karim, therefore, was at first surprised but not unduly distracted by the fact that the car in which he was travelling did not go directly to the Ministry of State Security office from which the New Revolution was being conducted, but instead appeared to be heading north-west and away from the Nile. Soon Cairo was left behind without the car being stopped for more than a second or two at any of the numerous road blocks which had been set up *en route*. But gradually this began to be disturbing, and once they were on the desert road, the Sheik demanded to be told their destination in a stiff and formal manner, as befitted the role he was playing.

'Alexandria,' came the reply. 'Your Excellency has shown such interest in naval affairs that you are to be the guest of the Egyptian Navy.'

The news of her son's murder struck Micheline with the force of a thunderclap. She and Pemberton had not been close. Indeed, since his Harvard days they had only seen each other at long intervals and then only because of a sense of duty on either side. They had never liked each other, and of all her husbands she had had less regard for Pemberton's father than for any of the others.

Nevertheless a son is a son. That could never be changed, and when the news was broken to her by General Sayyid she collapsed. General Sayyid, as part of the plan, had 'disappeared' so far as the world was concerned. In fact, and with her cognisance, he had taken over her Alexandria house, deftly removing her own servants into safe custody, where they would be held incommunicado till the crisis was resolved, and replacing them with a specially picked staff of his own.

This part of the plan, he told her, would be known to Major Masri, but it would not be revealed to Mustapha Khaliq and the PITO force. It also appeared to be the sum total of the information available to Micheline when the use of her house had been requested. She had agreed to this private reservation, because she knew that this was what Henri would have wanted, without asking further questions at the time. In Egyptian politics she had found it better to keep things at arm's length whenever possible. She had not pressed her curiosity until now. Pemberton's murder, however, changed all that. Now she would take a hand in the game herself.

'All I can tell you, Micheline,' Sayyid murmured in his most sympathetic tone, 'is that Pemberton was never one of us, he was never a part of *our* side of the plan. He should never have got himself in the firing line.'

'Then who put him there?'

'He did work for both sides. It's always a risk.'

'Oh, God!' Micheline said. 'Oh, my God . . .'

'You know I would have stepped in had I had the slightest idea that this might happen. But you know how things are – especially here. When an action starts you can no longer control front-line troops from the base.'

'Front-line troops!' she said with the utmost contempt. 'A gang of cheap Mafiosi even Henri would think twice about mixing with. You Egyptians . . .'

'Well,' said the General with a twitch of the shoulders, 'I'm not so sure about that. Your husband is the man who hands out the money.'

'Nonsense. He may have done so once or twice in the past. That was simply a matter of business – of international banking. You know that. In any case the Phalangists have got him in Beirut. You know perfectly well he's been out of it for the last ten days.'

'This operation is somewhat older than ten days, my dear. I'm afraid Henri was – and is – very considerably involved.' He went and put his arm round her shoulder. 'But recrimination is not going to help. I'm exceedingly sorry it happened.'

'*You*'re sorry,' she said bitterly, 'he was *my* son.'

She began to cry in a way she had forgotten since a girl. Sayyid watched her compassionately. On a personal level they were fond of each other. This mutual affection had grown from an almost casual affair, one of many in both their lives, and was based on the fact that from either side of the sexual divide they looked out on the world with much the same intelligence, will power and determination to get the most out of whatever engaged their attention. Both were predators: both had a high regard for power and both above all enjoyed their lives, the present moment excepted. But just as they had come together casually, so now they had drifted apart. Ships in the night.

'I wish I'd never said yes to your rotten little plan,' she said letting anger take the place of her tears. 'It was doomed from the start.'

'It's not a rotten little plan. It's not doomed, and what is more you don't know what it is.'

'I can guess.'

'We can all do that.'

The General looked coldly into the distance. A silence ensued which Micheline found oddly difficult to break. So she tossed her head impatiently and then went off on a new tack.

'Bloody Russians,' she said. 'I told Henri not to get involved. I warned him right at the start.'

'Unfortunately that's easier said than done. These days we all have to get involved – or they involve us. It's a calculated risk. And if there's one thing your husband can do better than most, it's work out a risk.'

'And did you calculate on having my son murdered?'

'That's not a reasonable thing to say.'

'Try being me,' she snapped, 'and see how reasonable you feel.'

She sat for a while in silence gradually getting herself together.

'And the President?' she asked in the end. He avoided her eyes.

'You could say everyone is safe when they're dead,' he murmured.

'Oh, my God!' Micheline cried out. 'You haven't done *that*?'

'I haven't done anything,' he went on, still avoiding her eyes, 'except to survive. I did under King Farouk and I did under President Nasser. A storm is a storm. You'd better come to terms with that fact yourself. I can't protect you for ever. I tell you these things get out of control.'

He shrugged his shoulders, and then glanced at her in a cold hard way.

'Until the ones that matter are safe in the bag. We're only doing to them what they planned to do to us. We took over their operation, turned it around and started it a day early. That's basically what has happened. Forty-eight hours should be enough to see who is loyal and who is not. Then we all come out of hiding again.'

'And suppose it goes wrong?'

'Suppose it doesn't go wrong,' Sayyid said crisply, 'that way we're more likely to stay alive ourselves.'

'And you trust Masri?'

She knew he would never return a direct answer to a direct question of that kind and, as expected, a smoky look seemed to drift into his eyes. He smiled gently and said, 'Trust no one until you see how the man in question reacts. Power is what matters. Look what has happened next door in Libya.' He paused for a moment to let this sink in. 'Masri has been playing with that same kind of fire for a very long time, longer than he thinks we know. In fact, he takes the situation here in Egypt to be far more simple than it is. The next forty-eight hours will tell.'

Lars Sweeney's instinct had been right. The car sent to fetch Andrea took her not to General Sayyid but to the New Revolutionary Headquarters. Whilst not openly under arrest, it became clear to Andrea that she would have a hard time getting away unless and until whoever was giving the orders declared her to be no longer required. On arrival at Major Masri's Command Post she was put in a small room with a barred window looking out on an inner courtyard. The room had a bare table and two hard chairs, but otherwise indistinguishable from a prison cell.

'Wait here,' the young officer told her, 'Major Masri will send for you when it is convenient to see him.'

'It is General Sayyid I've come to see.'

'You will see whoever Major Masri decides you should see,' the officer said curtly and left the room.

'So!' she said to herself, and sat down on one of the wooden chairs. Unlike Mado she had had little experience of being held captive before. This was a comparatively new treat and certainly not one she would wish to repeat. She stared out of the window and tried to order her thoughts. There had been better days in her life.

After about an hour, during which time her bottom had become numb through sitting on the cushionless chair and she had taken to pacing up and down the small room, an orderly of some kind threw open the door, glared at her and said, 'You! Follow me!'

She did as she was told. She was then led through that kind of meaningless bustle in the corridors which elsewhere she had always associated with political crisis of one sort or another, disturbances in which no one quite knew who was who nor exactly what was going on. Only one fact became glaringly clear: the New Revolution appeared to be an all-male affair.

Clad as she was in jeans, she received looks ranging from disdain through rape to plain outright hostility. These looks were backed up by sneers in a language she did not understand. The various soldiers and civilian Egyptians who stood around morosely smoking, or who were trundling about in a self-important way, suggested only that they detested her for being female. Indeed, no other woman was to be seen. Then at last she found herself pushed into a bare but large room where Major Masri himself was sitting at a table covered with maps and papers. Another officer stood at his side. Neither smiled, nor was she invited to sit down although an empty chair had been left facing the table.

The Leader came straight to the point. He nodded at her in abrupt way.

'You have been chosen to help the New Revolution.'

'Have I indeed?'

Masri stopped, a look of slight surprise in his eyes.

'You do not wish to help?'

'I have no idea what you're talking about.'

'Your friend Mustapha Khaliq, with whom you were at Oxford University . . .'

'Oh, I see,' Andrea said. 'That's the way it is, is it?'

The man standing next to Major Masri said something to him in Arabic at which Masri nodded. There was a momentary pause as Masri appeared to be working something out in his mind. Then he jerked his head at the orderly who had brought her along and barked out an order. As the orderly grasped her roughly by the arm, Masri said, 'I have no time for this. Go and talk to the PITO leader.'

She was then unceremoniously manhandled out of their presence into an Army truck and, after a short jerky journey, prodded – or rather goosed, as she later described it – into another decayed, dirty building identical in its complement of smoking, sulky, scowling men to the Masri headquarters. This was the PITO Command Post.

By now the anger she had felt initially had seeped down into the kind of senseless frustration which spreads around an airport departure hall when news of yet another delay has just been announced. Revolutions, she reflected ruefully, are for those who make them.

She found it hard to imagine how she might be called on

to help this current nonsense in Cairo. Whilst waiting on Mustapha Khaliq's pleasure, she thought back to their last encounter in Rome, when PITO had abducted Elissa Marides for a high ransom. From the PITO point of view that endeavour had failed. However, thinking it over, she forced herself to admit that Cairo might well be different. Terrorists were much more likely to have a better run for their money on the banks of the Nile.

This train of thought came sharply to an end with her being hustled into the room where Mustapha Khaliq was seated alone. He waved her to a chair. No smile, but at least a recognition of who she was – perhaps even of a past relationship.

'I'm sorry to inconvenience you in this way,' he began as if they were both in some Oxford don's room, 'but time is short. Yesterday you saw the late President.'

'Late?' Andrea said, startled, 'You haven't . . . God! you disgust me, you lot.'

'Indeed?' Khaliq remarked, as if totally unmoved. 'And since when have you changed your spots?' He paused fractionally, and then went on firmly. 'However, we have no time for dialectic. Here is the profile, article or whatever you call it, which you wrote as a result of that interview. Read it. Sign it and then you'll be told how next you can help.'

'But I haven't . . .' Andrea faltered and then stopped, realising the pointlessness of such a remark. Her one-time Oxford companion then handed over some typewritten sheets and indicated that she should read them there and then. In passing she thought it just as well she had been allowed to sit down, since when she did begin to study the document, she felt dizzy and could well have fallen over.

The piece she was supposed to have written turned out to be a scathing, propagandist attack on the President, accusing him of everything from corruption to unnatural practices. This was the full Marxist apologia for the New Revolution. All the old clichés, the lies and the double-think. All the old nauseating trash. When she reached the end of it, she looked up into the PITO leader's stony eyes.

'Well?' said Mustapha Khaliq impatiently. He clapped his hands and a tough-looking young woman whose backside was unsuitable for the khaki jeans she wore, strode into the room and took up a position near to Andrea. The face was vaguely familiar. She must have been on the last operation in Rome.

'I could never have written this,' Andrea said. 'My editor would only have to read the first paragraph to know this is a fake.'

'Then change it to the way you would write it. You have half an hour.'

'I'm sorry,' Andrea said, 'I couldn't possibly do that.'

'Don't waste my time. We both know you *will* see your way to doing what we ask,' Khaliq said, lighting a cigarette and stressing the word 'will' in the lightest way. 'In any event the piece will be sent to your paper under your name. In the meantime, you will remain here. There is other material I wish you to study. It will help you explain the New Revolution to the West.'

'Thank you,' Andrea said, 'but no.'

The words were scarcely out of her mouth when Khaliq murmured 'Ephrosini!' and nodded at the woman, who stepped up and gave Andrea two stinging slaps on her face. This took Andrea completely by surprise, and despite herself she cried out in pain and caught her breath in a sob. The shock effect was increased because, illogically, Andrea had not expected physical assault from a woman. From one of the slobs outside, yes, from this large and quite attractive girl, no. Then for good measure she received a third terrible slap.

'Remove her,' Khaliq said to Ephrosini, 'and do not take too long to make her see sense.'

Two male thugs came in swiftly and wrenched her brutally out of the room. Then it was down a couple of flights of stairs, and yet again through the dreary crowd of nondescript irregulars staring at her swollen face and red eyes and making, she supposed, insolent, obscene remarks in Arabic. Finally she was thrown with force into a cellar room lit by a single low-wattage bulb. She collapsed gasping on the stone floor to the sound of a key turning in a lock.

If the atmosphere in the Russian Embassy had been tense when Tarnham had left to see Major Masri, it thickened explosively once it became known that he had not turned up at New Revolutionary Headquarters.

'So where is he?' General Simonov demanded aggressively of Colonel Karai whose face now seemed to have taken on a permanent shade of yellow-white. Karai did not reply, except for a slight raising of the eyebrows.

'Answer!' Simonov barked out. 'You are the liaison between the New Revolution and ourselves. Where is the Sheik?'

'The Cairo traffic is a factor which must have been underestimated in the plan.'

'Are you attempting some English joke? You consider the Sheik would allow himself to be held up in a traffic jam? He could have walked there by now.'

'Are we sure he has not arrived? After all you were tricked into releasing Mado on false information that I had been snatched.'

'Now you accuse me?' The General was very angry indeed.

'No, Comrade General. But the fact was that I *had* been held up in the traffic.' He shrugged his shoulders to underline his contempt.

'Intentionally held up. You were fooled. You are always being fooled. You *are* a fool.'

They detested each other. Moreover, each had private fears suspected, but not precisely identified, by the other, the only common certainty they shared being a clear knowledge of what would happen to the pair of them if and when they were known to have failed.

'Why has Masri not honoured his pledge? The Fleet is still lying off and not anchored inside Alexandria.'

'I presume he is waiting for the Sheik to arrive.'

'You presume,' the General said scornfully. 'You will soon be presuming in another place if this part of the plan misfires. I can assure you of that.'

There seemed to be no answer to that, so Karai relapsed into his Number Two Attitude of Dumb Insolence. He consoled himself that one of these days, when they were back in Moscow, there would be a 4 a.m. knock on the General's door, followed by a swift ride in a curtained car to the Lubyanka – the last official ride his hated superior would take as a General of the KGB. That, Karai, was almost sure, had been arranged. And yet . . .

And yet, if something *had* happened to the Sheik here in Cairo, then it was equally possible that he, Karai, might not see Moscow again, except with himself under arrest. Both these senior officers of the KGB were on front line duty in an operation of paramount importance to the Soviet State. They had to succeed. Karai had long been too much of a realist not to appreciate that it lay fully within the General's prerogative simply to ring the bell on his desk and have his subordinate removed to a cell in the embassy, stripped of his power and made instantly as helpless as he, Karai, intended the General one day to be. Although Karai never drank except in the line of duty, today, when he regained the privacy of his own office, he poured himself out a Comrade-sized vodka there and then. He was not having a nice time at all.

Had it not been for the Revolution and the growing number of crises it seemed to provoke, Mado would have enjoyed the visit he was paying to the Modern Touristic Hotel. The building itself could be considered modern to the year 1890, and the décor of ancient palm and discoloured marble reminded Mado of similar pre-World War II establishments, such as the Sphinx in Paris.

The hotel made but little pretence to serve any other purpose than that for which it had been built, and which it had ably and obviously fulfilled for some eighty years. It sported a French lift of exiguous size on which the maintenance might well be in arrears. Although it added a charm of its own to the entrance hall, apart from bringing the girls and their clients into close vertical contact on their way up to the room, it struck Mado that the lift would be a hazard it would be better to avoid. Moreover, as the bar took up most of the ground floor level and Mado was not minded to avail himself of the facilities on offer in the upper part of the hotel, an invitation to ride in the lift could safely be refused.

'You like the hotel?' Abdul said. 'Up-to-date décor? The fittings – very good. Modern.'

Mado guessed that the taxi-driver would be likely to have some financial interest in the business activities of the establishment.

'Some of the ladies look quite post-war too,' Mado said with a smile. 'Yes, Abdul, it's much to my taste. One point, though, how do we go on for news of the outside world?'

Abdul's knowing look indicated that he realised Mado was fully on the ball.

'Hafiz the barman has a wireless set over there by the ice box.'

Mado saw that this was indeed true. The Hafiz set had an elegant fretwork front plus two coils on top. No doubt it was a superheterodyne job with valves which needed time to warm up.

'Hafiz will tell us anything important that is announced,' Abdul went on. 'Hafiz is a friend of Mr Sammy at the Club

Al Fayoum. In fact when he is not at the club, Mr Sammy often visits us here.'

'Ah!' said Mado, and ordered two large Scotch. But as soon as he had tasted the drink, he made a face and returned it to Hafiz, demanding a more genuine product and not something which, Mado claimed, had undoubtedly been distilled in a Khalifa dustbin. The local product, however, seemed acceptable to Abdul who also appeared to be undisturbed by the Prophet's veto on the use of alcohol. Hafiz grinned craftily and replaced Mado's drink.

'I see the effendi appreciates quality,' he murmured, 'please to excuse innocent mistake.'

'What now?' Mado asked Abdul. Normally such surroundings would have put him completely at ease, and he could have analysed the situation at his leisure. Today, however, the crisis outside seemed to press in on the dimly lit bar like a thick cloud of uncertainty, restlessness and fear.

'The effendi was a friend of Mr Pemberton Fuller?' Abdul enquired.

'I met him for the first time last night and then only for a moment or so.'

Abdul looked at his feet.

'It is always dangerous to serve two masters.'

'Or, as you yourself suggested earlier on, three or four masters, Abdul. Especially when you have a complicated situation like there seems to be in Cairo today.'

They studied each other in a guarded but not unfriendly way.

'I know something of the effendi's career. Permit me to offer sincere respect.'

'Well, thank you, Abdul. That's always nice to hear. Now what practical use can I put that to in this beautiful modernistic bar?'

'Ah! effendi is making a joke...'

'Perish the thought, Abdul. I was trying to find out what

suggestions you might have for any next move I should make.'

'I do not know what the effendi is trying to do,' Abdul said, sweeping the gloom with his dark eyes. 'I understand effendi is in Cairo on behalf of 'o kyrios Marides and not directly for British Intelligence.'

'But I seem to have been somewhat overtaken by events. For instance the late Pemberton Fuller had something he was trying to tell us or sell us last night. Perhaps rather foolishly we turned him away a little too soon.'

'We?' Abdul said.

'I have an American friend.'

'Of course. Mr Lars Sweeney, is it not?'

Again Mado was privately astonished at how much Abdul seemed to know.

'Yes.'

Abdul began to speak and then stopped, obviously feeling for words. Eventually he said, 'People who work for super powers do sometimes make mistakes. Because of arrogance, we sometimes consider, here in Egypt. All that power behind both the KGB and the CIA – it spells danger, sir, does it not? That is, if you come too close to it.'

Mado nodded. 'Now, Abdul, the next question is: do you think your Hero of the Crossing, your actual Major Masri, will succeed with his coup?'

'Has he not done so already?'

'Ah! Then let me put it another way. How long will he last?'

Abdul smiled and looked away into the distance. 'To use another up-to-date phrase, if I may, sir. That is the sixty-four thousand dollar question.'

'I agree,' Mado said, 'but I'm asking the questions, Abdul, and you are supplying the answers.'

He signed at Hafiz to bring another round of drinks.

'As to how long anyone lasts in Cairo, sir, that depends on

the KGB and the CIA, does it not? Of course, if the President were to return . . .'

'You don't think he's been assassinated?'

'Not by Major Masri,' Abdul said with unexpected directness, 'on that I would lay a wager. However, there are others. Major Masri may not have all the support he is counting upon. When a chairman goes there is always a power struggle. There are men close to Major Masri . . .'

'Such as Mustapha Khaliq?'

Abdul nodded.

'International terrorists, effendi. They are well organised these days. If they have not killed him, they will have the President somewhere well-hidden. If they can keep him away from the scene of events long enough to secure themselves in power – then who knows what will happen? We may even have our friends the Russians back here in strength.'

'And that depends on how successful Sheik Karim al Hammad may be in influencing the situation, does it not?'

Abdul froze for a moment, as if he had received an electric shock. Then he said carefully, 'I see now what it is the effendi is trying to achieve.'

A pause ensued. Both men looked at each other and then away. Eventually Mado broke the silence.

'I wonder if you do. I have a personal interest, of course, but . . .'

Again Abdul smiled. 'But you are really asking to what extent is the Sheik in control?'

'Exactly.'

'If we knew that, effendi, we would not be sitting here now.' He paused as each thought out the implications. 'It is the international terrorists – in this case PITO – Mustapha Khaliq – that really make things happen,' Abdul continued. 'They do the heavy work, do they not?'

'You are saying the tail wags the dog?'

'They do the capturing and the killing. Of course the KGB

pay, but then so will the CIA. However, with someone like Mustapha Khaliq, money has never been the factor which really matters. Money can always be obtained.' He made a gesture of slight contempt. 'Libya or Iraq will always oblige PITO if the Russians or the Americans – or even yourselves and the French – make too many awkward demands.'

'And suppose I wanted to remove the Sheik from the current scene?'

'That is far beyond the power of a mere taxi-driver, effendi, and you would probably need a very great deal of money. But wait, here is Mr Sammy! I thought he might look in. He would be a better person to consult on a proposition of such importance. Ah! but perhaps at a later date . . .' he added, with a new note of warning in his voice.

Mado looked up and across the room. As Abdul had remarked, the owner of the Club Al Fayoum could be observed making his way to another part of the bar, accompanied to Mado's surprise by Ephrosini-Graziella, the late Pemberton Fuller's girlfriend, and the only woman whom Mado knew to be a close confidante of the leader of the Pan Islamic Terrorist Organisation.

'Let's take a drink off them,' Mado said, getting down from his bar stool. Abdul held him back with a gentle tug on his sleeve.

'The effendi knows the lady accompanying Mr Sammy?' Abdul asked in a cautionary tone of voice.

'Perhaps better than you do, Abdul. Although it was long ago when she was still a student in Beirut.'

'She has changed since then. No longer a student.'

'Yes, Abdul, that I know too.'

He walked across the room, remembering Graziella and her beautiful rounded buttocks all those years ago when they had first made it together on a lonely Lebanese beach. The girl had been an eager and sensuous lay, but Mado also recalled her suppressed anger and tears on the way back into Beirut, when he had told her quietly that he knew she had recently been recruited into the Communist party and had only allowed herself to be seduced by him for an ulterior and ideological motive. Since then she had totted up quite a score, hardening in the process into what seemed to Mado to be the archetype of the mid-seventies girl terrorist in jeans, the days of innocence long, long forgotten in the cynical slanging and banging which her received ideas must have forced upon her mind.

Now, as he nodded at Mr Sammy, she greeted him in a cold, hostile way. He saw she had a gun discreetly hidden by one of the folds of her still voluptuous body, and no doubt she would be remembering their last brush with each other in Rome, when for a time she had been ordered to act as Elissa Marides's gaoler, with orders to kill if need be.

'Hal*lo*!' Mado called out to Sammy with a watchful nod to the girl. 'How nice of you to ask us over for a drink. You know my friend, Abdul, of course?'

For a second or two he thought Sammy was going to take it the wrong way and be tedious. Then came the flicker of a smile as Sammy made a sign to Hafiz the barman.

'I see you have in no way lost your nerve, Mr Mado.'

'I don't know about that,' Mado said. 'I'm getting a bit old for the sort of pleasures I had last night after leaving your lovely club. Incidentally, why are you closed today?'

'You haven't heard the news? There is something we call a revolution in progress.'

'Good heavens,' Mado said, with a wink at Graziella to which she reacted by turning her head angrily away, 'whatever next? Interferes with business, I take it?'

'And what can Sammy the Wog do for you today, Mr Mado? Have you thought of any of those questions you want answered?'

'As a matter of fact, I have,' Mado said, 'although I don't think I want to ask them here and now.' He addressed himself to Graziella, 'And how is the Renta Terrorist Group these days? Blooming, I hope. Yes. Ah, well, you seem to be more gorgeously attractive than ever, my love. I always think it such a pity your boss doesn't interest himself in the ladies, does he?'

'I should be more careful, if I were you,' Sammy said with a crooked smile, 'you are not on privileged territory here, Mr Mado, not as you would be in the Club Al Fayoum.'

A khaki-clad soldier of some kind appeared at the door, caught Ephrosini's eye and jerked his head towards the street. Without another word the gropeable Miss Buttocks, as Mado thought of her, put down the soft drink she was about to raise to her lips, instinctively felt for the gun tucked into her jeans and, with a quick withering look at Mado, strode out of the room. Mado watched her go and then turned back to the bar. Sammy the Wog was still favouring him with his ominous smile.

'That's a beautiful arse,' Mado said, 'such a pity that other parts of the outfit seem to be out of kilter, such as the head, for instance, or the soul if she has such a thing . . .'

'Mr Mado, if you have questions you'd like to ask, why don't we go over there in the corner where we can be by ourselves?'

'A good idea,' Mado said, and turned away – at which moment he received a stunning blow at the base of the neck, lost consciousness and slumped to the floor.

8

By now, some forty-eight hours after news of the revolution had first broken to the world, a great confusion reigned in Cairo. This differed in many ways from the chaos of Beirut. In Cairo the military still appeared to be in control. It is true there were sporadic reports of odd shootings, but these were few and far between. People still walked about Cairo. Taxis and private cars seemed largely to have disappeared and public transport, never notably efficient, had now come to a standstill.

But except for an initial run on the food shops, life appeared to be comparatively normal. True, there were barricades manned by soldiers who demanded to see identity cards for reasons only known to themselves – but then, barricades were always apt to spring up overnight in the Middle East. Ordinary folk kotowed as necessary and went on their way. Shops that could shutter themselves did so but remained open to those who knocked.

Older people claimed to be able to see similarities to the early days of the Neguib/Nasser regime, but no one paid much attention to such old wives' tales. However, there was a considerable anxiety in the air. Moreover this tension increased with every hour that passed in the absence of a public appearance by the President or any of his close advisers. Where was the Head of State? The entire government seemed to have been spirited away – and this, in fact, was what had happened.

Major Masri's voice could be heard regularly on the radio,

but television remained off the air. The Major was telling everyone to keep calm, to await events and to stay at home. Suitable announcements would soon be made. But the hours passed into days and still nothing definite was known. As yet there were few signs of panic, but an overall feeling did exist that it would not be long before the scene darkened.

No newspapers were on sale and all frontiers remained firmly and effectively closed. The popular explanation was that there had been a Palace revolution and a general cleaning-up of corruption was being put into operation. No one paid much attention to that. What, however, had happened to their generally popular President? People did not swarm out on to the streets as they had done on Nasser's death, but everyone knew that that this kind of haphazard, possibly undirected, hiatus would not, indeed could not, continue for ever. And who could be sure that the Israelis might not again be tempted to seize their chance?

The communication units of foreign embassies in Cairo, of course, worked overtime and such intelligence as could be grubbed up went out through these channels. But set against the world situation as it was in 1976, the Masri revolt quickly took on the look of a low key affair. This opinion was strengthened by a total absence of television news units, and by the fact that the few media men who did manage to slip in illicitly found that they could not work. And after all, as the world said these days, if it wasn't on the telly it could scarcely matter at all.

So much then for the outer scene in Cairo, the scene which other countries knew about through their embassies, the scene which would wind up as a couple of lines or at most a paragraph in the Almanacs for the year. A somewhat trivial event . . .

Behind this frontage, however, intense activity prevailed amongst and between Gaddafi, Assad, Brezhnev, Ford and whoever it was who was theoretically governing Great Britain at that time. In those circles even the smallest attempt to alter the Egyptian *status quo* became at once the opposite of a low key affair. These attitudes were, in turn, reflected into the embassies of the countries concerned in Cairo, so that tension all the time continued to rise like water behind a dam which might at any moment overflow or begin to spring a leak.

A whole day had now passed since Lars Sweeney had last seen Mado and Andrea and he had taken to commuting between the American Embassy, the Hilton bar and the various establishments owned or used by the CIA. Nowhere could he glean any news of his two British friends. Both had simply disappeared without a trace.

Since the racing at Gezira had also been abandoned, Lars found time a little heavy on his hands. He continued to exhibit his usual bland exterior to the world, but behind it anxiety grew. He had come to rely on George Mado suddenly and silently showing up at his side in the Hilton bar, a glass of whisky in his hand, to be followed a little later by Andrea Eckersley's casually elegant arrival across the crowded room, and the subsequent exchange of news and information which all three had separately gleaned.

Now that Lars Sweeney, like Mado, no longer held a direct security brief which would tie him in to a given part of a set operation, he felt from time to time disorientated, as Mado had done. Even though security work in the field inevitably requires a Job-like patience in the 'waiting about' process, Lars Sweeney had come not only to appreciate but also to count on the presence of fellow workers in the vineyard.

He had just started on his fourth vodka on the rocks that morning when a message was brought to him in the bar. The letter had evidently been delivered by hand. The colour was deep blue, the writing paper hand-made and from it exuded a faint but expensive scent.

'Dear Mr Sweeney,' the firm, feminine script declared, 'we

haven't met before but I think we should. Please come as soon as you can. Do not phone.' There was no address but the signature was 'Micheline Bariolet'. He slipped the letter into his pocket and thought hard for a moment or so.

Was this purely and simply a trap? If so, it appeared somewhat ingenuous at first sight. If not, then why had the approach been made in this pseudo-mysterious way? Why no address? Why the injunction not to telephone? Did the good lady imagine him to be new to the realities of the Cairo telecommunications system? In that event could she herself be ignorant of his own deeper connections? Finally, if *that* were so why would she want to get in touch with him at all?

He finished his drink, put down his glass and stood up. Whilst aware of being under surveillance to a greater or lesser degree, a quick glance round the room now convinced him – and at the same time struck a chill into his solar plexus – that the watch had been strengthened. It would be advisable, he decided, to make the embassy his first port of call.

If Lars Sweeney had begun to feel somewhat alone and stuck out on a limb in the Hilton bar, it was nothing to what was going on in the Russian Embassy.

'This is preposterous!' General Simonov shouted, and then relieved his feelings by adding an army oath from the Second World War. 'What do you mean, the Navy refuses to release him? Is Masri Leader of the Revolution or is he not?'

Colonel Karai and General Sayyid's son, who had long ago tried and failed to get out of the liaison job he had been given, stood strictly to attention in front of Simonov's desk. Both were a beige colour in complexion and looked as though they had not slept for days, which was true. Neither answered.

'Well?' Simonov went on, banging his clenched fist down on the desk. 'Is he or isn't he?'

'He is Leader of the Revolution,' Sayyid's son said.

'But he is not completely in command of the situation,' Karai added. 'No doubt if he were to go to Alexandria himself, he might regain control, but the Egyptian Navy has decided to become a law to itself.'

'Then they must be forced to obey,' Simonov interrupted angrily. 'Where is Mustapha Khaliq? He was ordered to be here.'

'He did not see fit to come,' Karai said, 'and we have no means of making him.'

'Then go there yourself and direct him to keep to his agreement.'

'If I do that, Comrade General, I might not be allowed to return.'

This seemed to pull Simonov up with a jerk. Privately he thought this a sound idea, but outwardly he showed no trace of his feelings.

'So?' he demanded of Sayyid's son. 'Do we now have a revolution within a revolution? Is that how it is?'

The young man shrugged his shoulders, a gesture which infuriated Simonov even more. The KGB General took a turn up and down the room. Then he came to the nub of the matter.

'*When* is the invitation to our fleet going to be made? And don't shrug your shoulders again. Did you ask Major Masri that specific question?'

'Yes, sir, I did.'

'And what was his answer?'

'The Arabic is difficult to translate.'

'What did he say?' Simonov yelled.

'Yimkin tala mish-mish,' young Captain Sayyid replied, keeping as straight a face as he could.

'And what does that mean?'

'Literally, "when the apricots ripen". It's another way of saying he doesn't know.'

'Doesn't know! Doesn't know! No wonder the Israelis can walk over you whenever they choose.'

'The Israelis did not do that in the October war,' Sayyid said proudly.

'The October war!' Simonov said scornfully. 'Everything comes back sooner or later to that damned October war. What about now? Eh? What about now?'

'Comrade General,' Karai said, 'with respect, shouting about it will not get us the action we want.'

'You realise, Colonel, what failure to get the action we want is likely to do to your personal career?'

'To all our careers, Comrade General,' Karai answered, a glint in his eye.

'I shall go and see Masri myself,' Simonov said, 'and you will come with me, Captain Sayyid. Colonel Karai, you will stay here.'

'As the Comrade General decides,' Karai said, allowing himself a trace of a smirk. 'And will you go on to see the PITO leader?'

'Perhaps. Perhaps not.' Simonov said, nodding a dismissal to his hated subordinate.

Karai saluted smartly and left the General's office. He had a report on General Simonov to prepare for secret and independent submission to Moscow.

There were still a few taxis to be found outside the Hilton and Lars Sweeney decided to take one to the American Embassy. If Micheline Bariolet wished their meeting to be secret, he would have to reach the mansion on the banks of the Nile undetected and to do this he would need to devise some way of shaking off his surveillance. Whilst he was working this out, the taxi driver broke into his train of thought.

'Effendi make trip to the Pyramids?'

'Thank you, Joe, but today is not a day for the Pyramids.'

'Special price. Camel ride included. Round trip. Square deal.'

'Sorry.'

'Effendi like modern touristic hotel: nice girls?'

'That, too, is out for today.'

'Perhaps effendi is interested in whereabouts of Mr Mado?' Abdul said, studying his face in the driving mirror.

'Ah,' said Lars, without the flicker of an eyelid, 'now we're on track again.'

He waited for Abdul to go on but a silence followed.

'Five hundred dollars,' Abdul said.

'Not worth it,' Lars said. 'I'll wait for the January sales. However, Joe . . .'

'Abdul.'

'However, Abdul, as you so obviously know where my interests lie perhaps we could do a deal about someone else.'

'Lady journalist?' Abdul said with a smile, 'British lady with hair the colour of sunset over western desert?'

'That's the one.'

'Two thousand dollar the pair.'

'Any discount for cash?'

'Effendi is joking . . .'

'You're damn right, I am. Pay two thousand dollars for a bum steer in a Cairo cab? Sure, I'm joking – and so are you. Who are you anyway?'

'My name is Abdul and I drive a taxi.'

'Well, Abdul,' Lars Sweeney said carefully, 'I'm glad about that.'

Another silence followed as they rattled on roughly in the direction of the embassy.

'America rich country,' Abdul said.

'You'll have to do better than that.'

'How, effendi?'

'Like come up with some kind of guarantee. Like both pieces of merchandise would be in good working order.'

'No guarantee. Information only, effendi.'

'No deal,' Lars said briefly. 'Delivery is the word for today. No delivery – no cash on the nail.'

'Effendi – so far as the lady is concerned, no one makes deals with PITO.'

'So that's where she is.'

'For Mr Mado, effendi will have to do rescue himself.'

'And then, when you have me in the trap as well, how much are you going to ask the next one along? The one who's going to rescue me?'

Abdul smiled and did not appear to mind being observed by Sweeney in this unusual facial expression. Somewhat to his surprise, Sweeney decided he was beginning to take to this pirate with his own particular brand of humour.

'America rich – so is Mr Marides.'

'Ah ha!' Lars said. 'I see the cut of your jib.'

'Your pardon, effendi?'

'I see where your train of thought is taking us.'

'You said to the American Embassy, sir, and here we are. Abdul wait?'

Sweeney gave him a long, hard look and then smiled himself.

'And I suppose Abdul knows where I'm headed next?'

There was the flicker of a nod.

'Sir – a suggestion...'

'Go ahead.'

'If effendi thinking of walking to next appointment, we say in Egypt better a lame camel than to walk yourself in the desert sun.'

'I don't imagine your camel is lame, Abdul. You also speak much better English than you want me to think you do.'

He was rewarded with another crafty smile revealing crooked teeth but undoubted charm.

'To use the effendi's own type of phrase – you're damn right!'

Sweeney began to get out of the taxi and then stopped, studying the other for a moment or so.

'Will you work for me, Abdul?'

'If I can.'

The answer came surprisingly quick.

'Well, can you? I mean will your other activities allow you to – to work on the side for me?'

'Effendi, I am Egyptian. We Egyptians have never been allowed to do much since the Mamalukes took us over. But, as I told Mr Mado, when all of you have gone, the pyramids remain. Leave the decision on how much I can do to me. I am on your side. But a man has to live.'

'I can see the problem. How does this grab you, Abdul? I promise you I won't be asking you to do anything against the real interests of Egypt.'

'How can the effendi promise any such thing? Who knows what real interests are? Now money is different again. Everyone knows where he is with money. Money is real.'

'How much do you want?'

'A very large sum.'

They stared hard at each other, thinking this out. Then Abdul said, 'Mr Marides can always claw it back from some other place. Death, however, is final.'

'No one's going to argue with that.'

Again there was a lengthy pause, each seeming to wait on the other.

'And you trust me, Abdul?'

'I trust you, effendi.'

'So, okay, let's give it a whirl.'

Instead of giving him the commercial smirk which Sweeney had half-expected, Abdul averted his eyes. For a moment or so he remained silent and sad. Indeed, had it been anyone else, Sweeney would have thought him on the point of tears.

'Very well,' Abdul eventually said in a low voice, 'let us see what can be done.'

He offered his hand and Sweeney shook it, surprised at the sensitive touch.

'Here is all I have in cash – three hundred dollars on account,' Lars Sweeney said and was further astonished when Abdul shook his head.

'Your hand is enough. But you must do what I advise. And don't delay.'

'If I am not here, a friend will take care of you.' With a nod, Sweeney slipped out of the cab and in through the embassy gate.

It took Lars Sweeney but a few minutes to clear what he called his 'Flight Plan' to the Bariolet mansion.

'The Watch on the Rhine seems to be better than we thought,' he remarked to the desk man in the embassy whose responsibility he had become, 'so in spite of Madame Bariolet's ban on the phone, I guess they'll find out where I am pretty soon. In fact they already know where I was headed.'

He did not have time to discover what the computer would say about Abdul, but he filled in the desk man briefly on what had happened to him since leaving the Hilton. He could programme the computer later on.

'Trust a Gyp taxi-driver? You crazy or something? Since when are lawyers romantic?' the desk man said sourly. He hated his present posting and longed to get back in the field himself. 'You realise they *have* assassinated the President?'

'Is that fact or just another read-out?'

'It's the balance of probability – the computer says.'

'So there's still no definite news?'

'They've turned Gaddafi back at the frontier. So Masri is still in control.'

'What's the word on the Russian Fleet?'

'Zero. But if they do enter Alexandria now the Sixth Fleet is likely to follow them in. So even if invited I guess it's no longer a local option. Have a good time with the banker's wife. The computer says her son was no loss to the world.'

'I don't suppose she wants to hear that,' Lars Sweeney said as he left. 'Let me have whatever there is on Abdul.'

'If you live that long,' the desk man said and went back to his work.

Outside on the corner there was no sign of Abdul; instead, another taxi was waiting.

'I take you, effendi,' the driver leaned over and called through the window. 'Abdul my friend.'

'Abdul, *my* friend,' Sweeney said. 'Where is he?'

He did not like this at all.

'Called back to headquarters. Abdul see you later tonight.'

Sweeney got into the cab. There was no point in hanging about.

'You know where to go?' he asked, watching the driver like a cat.

'Soleiman know where to go,' came the reply as the ancient Buick got under way. 'Soleiman *your* friend too.'

'It's great to have so many friends,' Sweeney said, wishing he had a gun. 'Good to know you, Soleiman.'

There were two new road blocks between the embassy and where the Bariolet house stood on the banks of the Nile, but at each of them Soleiman called out something in Arabic and they were waved through with a smile. After the second of these experiences, Sweeney asked how he did it.

'Soleiman own massage parlour, effendi. I say client in a hurry.'

'I wish I were – I mean to have a massage.'

'Take my card, effendi. To you special price.' He produced a luridly designed card from his pocket and passed it across. 'Unusual tastes catered for', it said.

'You work all the time with Abdul?' Sweeney asked as they

turned into the drive of the Bariolet mansion and the car stopped outside the imposing front door.

'Abdul my *friend*,' Soleiman answered, as if that settled the matter.

'How much do I owe you?' Sweeney said, getting out of the cab.

'One hundred dollars, effendi.'

'One hundred *dollars*?'

Soleiman nodded impassively, and then added for good measure, 'Abdul said to tell you – cheap at the price.'

'And so it is,' Sweeney said, coming to a quick decision and handing over the money. 'Don't wait – or you'll break the bank, my bank that is.'

Soleiman took the money, nodded again in a friendly fashion and then drove away at speed. There was now no one else in sight and Sweeney suddenly felt very much alone. He walked up the steps, cautiously looking around. As he reached the door and before he could ring the bell, it opened silently – almost eerily – and a white gallebeahed servant bowed him inside.

'This way, effendi,' he said and led him through the marble hall on to the terrace overlooking the garden and the Nile. Micheline rose to her feet from a wicker chair. She was wearing lemony-yellow slacks with a flimsy white top which showed off her breasts to better advantage, it struck Sweeney, than if she had been wearing nothing at all, which she certainly was underneath the top.

'It's vodka on the rocks, isn't it?' she said, dismissing the servant with a nod and offering her hand. 'I had it ready for you, so we needn't waste time.' Sweeney felt he could cap that remark, but instead merely shook her hand and then went across to the drinks table.

'Why was I not to call up? I seem to have half Cairo on my neck as it is.'

'The ones watching you are the goodies,' she said. 'We

don't know who listens in on the phone. It's as simple as that.'

'Well, *I'm* not sure who the goodies are,' he said, raising his glass to her without drinking and then added over the rim. 'Perhaps you can fill me in on that one.'

None of the drink passed his lips. She nodded.

'I'll try,' she said, 'but first tell me about Pemberton. You must have been one of the last people to see him.'

There was a catch in her voice and almost too quickly she fumbled a cigarette from a packet on the arm of her chair with a shaky hand. He did not think she was putting it on.

'It must have been a terrible shock.'

She nodded again.

'Do you have children, Mr Sweeney? Oh no, of course you don't, you're not married.'

'I was. As a matter of fact I have a grown-up daughter in California.'

'Well, there it is . . .' Micheline said. She gave her shoulders a twitch and this seemed to help her regain her poise. The picture of Andrea sitting in the same seat he was now in passed through his mind. He could see what a formidable lady Micheline could be if she chose, and on the spur of the moment he asked, 'What lay behind those interesting experiences you gave Andrea Eckersley the other night?'

'You fancy her, don't you, Mr Sweeney?'

'Right. Though I don't see what that has to do with the question.'

'I can understand that. She's a very attractive girl. As to that night – we had to find out how much she knew.'

'And did you?'

'Yes.'

'Who's the "we"?'

'Mr Sweeney, I asked you here to put the questions myself.'

'Maybe,' he said quietly, 'but you won't get any answers until you tell me who you are and what you're in the process of trying to achieve.'

She gave him the sort of smile it would be nice to wake up next to in the morning, and she then held the pause like the actress he knew her to be.

'How do you know I haven't put a Mickey Finn in your drink as well?' she said in a low slinky voice.

'Maybe you have – but then I'd have to drink it to find out, would I not? And I haven't.' He put down the glass. 'I thought you said, or implied, that we ought to save time.'

She laughed huskily. Once again Sweeney realised with a private pleasure what a magnificently sexual woman she was. No wonder Mado had used up his superlatives. They studied each other, Sweeney being certain that she was fully aware of how his blood was quickening and that it gave her pleasure too.

'It's all right,' she said, 'I was only putting you on. There's nothing but vodka in that glass.'

She reached over, took the glass and drank its contents herself, indicating that he should help himself to another.

'I can see why you've married four millionaires,' he said, doing as suggested, 'if you'll excuse the rather brash way of putting it.'

'I could probably excuse a great deal from you,' she said giving him another sultry look, which lasted even longer than before and which was so obvious it made him laugh, 'but you know all about me anyway – who I am and all that.'

'So okay, I know who you are.'

'And I've no doubt the many games I play – or some of them at least – have been fed into that computer you CIA-types love to play with. So what does the computer say I'm up to then?'

'It says you do a number of mutually contradictory things.'

'That's right. I'm a woman.'

'So is the computer in some of the answers it spews out.'

She laughed again.

'Spews out – I haven't heard that phrase for years. And that's not American either.'

'From Harvard I went on to Oxford,' Sweeney said, 'as well you know. Why don't we quit being skittish and get down to the facts?' She nodded and Sweeney went on, 'So why am I sitting here now?'

'You heard they killed the President?'

'Yes.'

'Do you believe it?'

'I'll believe anything for which there's a shred of evidence. Evidence of that particular event seems to be a little thin on the ground.'

'I think I know where the President is,' she said softly and gave him a long, steady look.

9

Mado regained consciousness in one of the more seedy rooms of the Modern Touristic Hotel. After a brief examination he seemed to himself to have suffered no lasting damage from the blow he had received. True, he had to admit to a nasty headache coupled with a burning thirst, but there was little unusual in that.

He had been laid out fully dressed on a dingy bed, and on first coming to, he spent a few idle moments examining his surroundings, none of which, he concluded, would stand exposure to any but the dimmest lights. The door had been locked. '*Mon Dieu!*' he addressed himself for some reason in a phoney French accent, 'ze great Poirot find heemself locked een a bordel against his veel.' Not that Poirot or anyone else could have done much about it, the way he felt, even had the most luscious of the ladies of the house been stretched out naked beside him. 'Zo vot vee do next?' he asked himself, looking at the door.

He fancied he could probably break down the door, but what after that? He walked about the room and then sat down on the bed with his head in his hands, trying to stop the pounding inside. The picture of Abdul, the taxi-driver, arose in his mind and with it the sad conclusion that once again he must have been tricked.

In fact, he had been led into a trap by allowing himself to be taken to the Modern Touristic Hotel, a trap then sprung by the arrival of Sammy the Wog. And yet, through it all, he still instinctively felt Abdul to be basically an okay man. There could be no doubt about Sammy the Wog, however – that one stood firmly on the hostile side.

The throbbing in his head had just begun to die down when he heard footsteps in the passage outside. Then a key turned in the lock and in came a man whom Mado took a moment or so to place. He carried a tray on which was a glass, a bottle of whisky and an old fashioned soda-water syphon contained in diamond-shaped lattice-work. The man also wore a smile on his face.

'My oh my!' Mado said. 'That's a welcome sight – and you are . . . ?'

'Hafiz barman, effendi. Compliments of Abdul. Abdul hopes effendi not too unwell.'

He poured out a generous measure of Scotch and offered it to Mado.

'Please to thank Abdul and say that apart from a steam hammer inside his head, the Sultan is in excellent fettle.'

'Abdul very sorry about what happened, effendi. Abdul claim not his fault. Abdul says effendi should not have approached Mr Sammy and the girl against his advice.'

'Well, there you go,' Mado said, 'Abdul was probably right. So how do I get out of here, Hafiz?'

'Abdul say effendi not try to escape. Bad for personnel of modern touristic hotel.'

'I see. And how does Abdul think it is for the effendi?'

Hafiz smiled. 'Abdul say "Our friends show us what we can do, our enemies teach us what we must do." Abdul is a friend. But he is not as strong as Mr Sammy. And then there is always the PITO. Effendi is a prisoner of PITO.'

'And you work for PITO?'

Hafiz shook his head. 'In Cairo today everyone works for the man who sticks gun in his back.'

Mado thought about this for a while. He could not fault the logic, but resented the fact that by any calculation he had suffered enough Middle Eastern tergiversation to last him a lifetime. Bovver, that's what it was.

'In other words if I escape, PITO will burn down the joint.'

'No, but they burn *us* – something like that, effendi,' then as Mado was about to speak, he hurriedly added, 'Abdul come back later. I think Abdul negotiate effendi's release.'

'And suppose he doesn't?'

Hafiz shrugged his shoulders.

'Modern touristic hotel much used by PITO. PITO gives orders. PITO store guns in basement. PITO keep prisoner's here.'

'Now that's interesting,' Mado said, thinking of the possibilities this opened up, 'and would there by any chance be an English lady prisoner here? A lady with red hair?'

'The colour of sunset over Western desert?'

'You could put it that way.'

'There might be.'

Hafiz had adopted the cautious expression of a merchant sitting cross-legged in the Souk, the sort of wary, bargaining look which Mado had frequently seen in Marides's eyes when the great Greek had been on the point of pulling off some especially dubious deal.

'Ah!' Mado said, suppressing a sigh of relief. 'And I suppose any further progress in that direction would be a matter of pounds and piastres, would it not?'

A Sphinx-like smile spread over the Egyptian's face.

'Effendi is a man of the world.'

'Leave the world out of this,' Mado said, pulling out his wallet. 'How much?'

A few minutes later, after a satisfactory figure had been agreed, Mado was taken along a corridor and down a floor into another room similar in every respect to the one in which he himself had been kept. Andrea was lying on the bed looking disconsolately at the ceiling.

'Half-hour I come back, effendi,' Hafiz said, locking the door from the outside. Andrea sat up, looked at Mado and smiled.

'I might have guessed it,' she said. 'What are you up to here?'

'Like the First Lady of Fleet Street, I was wondering what incredible piece of self-inflicted folly it was that got me into this mess – and after that how we're going to get out.'

'The folly that got *me* here,' Andrea said, 'was not to say yes at once to Mustapha Khaliq. So I suppose I'm being cooled off.'

She told him of her interview with Masri and Khaliq, and Mado in turn passed on what he had just learnt from Hafiz the barman.

'The Modern Touristic Hotel is a PITO prison and arms dump,' Mado said, 'and the interesting question for now is why they bother to keep us here at all. A couple of bullets would be altogether cheaper and quicker.'

'They only want us out of the way – not for ever, but now. A man like Khaliq never for a moment doubts that people such as you and I will come round to a correct point of view in the end. I've heard him call it PITO's historical imperative. Khaliq is quite certain I can be reformed and that he's the man to do it.'

'I always had a notion you were a Marxist underneath, Mado said, watching her warily.

'Well, I'm certainly not a Tory,' she tossed her head in annoyance, 'but whatever I am, it's not for Khaliq and his gang of assassins. Anyway this is no time for political theory, George Mado, your job is to get us out of here.'

'Yes, ma'am,' Mado agreed, thinking what a very attractive woman she was, even bedraggled and tousled as she now seemed to be – or maybe it was *because* she was bedraggled and tousled that at present she appealed to him more than when she was her more usual 'got up' self. The protective instinct in a man is a very dangerous lever to pull, he said to himself and when Andrea said 'Yes' and smiled, he realised that he had begun to pick up his old habit of speaking his thoughts aloud, a habit of which he had imagined himself cured after the scrapes it had got him into on the previous operation in Rome.

'So stop feeling protective,' Andrea said, 'and do something about it.'

Mado walked to the window, pushed aside the dirty muslin curtain and looked down on to a small dark inner courtyard. Two floors below there seemed to be a glass roof over some salon or hall. There was also a convenient drainpipe just outside the window, though from what Mado remembered of Egyptian construction work it might be a chancy business to rely on that for support.

'Here,' Mado said with a winning smile, 'you're an athletic girl . . .'

'Down that pipe? Like hell I do.'

'You can follow me when I reach that ledge down there,' Mado said, swinging out and clutching the drainpipe. 'Once a Boy Scout . . .'

With a surprising agility he was shinning down the pipe before she could stop him.

'Nothing to it,' he called up, and almost without thinking she followed him down on to the ledge. On one side was a window similar to the one in the room they had left: on the other lay the flat stained-glass roof which would certainly not support one person's weight, let alone the pair of them.

'We'd better climb in here,' Mado said, attempting to prise open a window which was covered on the inside, like the one up top, with a half-drawn muslin curtain which at one time might have been white.

Mado peered in through the window, trying to see if the room were similar in every respect to the one two floors up, and concluded it was. He could certainly make out a bed and from the shape of what was on it, it seemed to be in use. This was further confirmed by an angry feminine voice calling out in alarm from inside the room, no doubt startled by the apparitions at the window. Then, at that moment, the ledge on which they were standing collapsed and both were pitched out, down and through the glass roof.

Some instinct must have operated in both of them, since in falling they curled up as far as possible and plummeted through the glass like two large cannon balls. Beneath the glass roof stood an outsized four-poster bed, the top of which broke their fall and they ended up shaken but unhurt on the bed itself. This luckily proved to be unoccupied and appeared to have been set up on some sort of dais. The rest of the salon had been filled with rows of chairs, and the only other piece of furniture was an old fashioned umbrella stand incongruously stacked with various whips and thongs. They were alone.

'How about that, then?' Mado observer, picking himself up and helping Andrea to extricate herself from a few pieces of glass which were still sticking to her clothing. 'Trust Mado to land in the "Feelthy Exhibition" room. Are you all right?'

'I think so.'

'Let's get moving then.'

Mado tried the door which was locked. However, the crash had already begun to cause its own repercussion, and they could hear excited shouting from elsewhere in the building together with footsteps in the corridor outside. Mado gestured to Andrea to stand behind him so that when the door did open it would shield them until whoever was entering became visible. They did not have long to wait.

A key turned quickly in the lock and the next thing Mado saw a gun and a brown forearm advancing into the room. Without further ado Mado chopped his own hand down on the arm, which he grasped. The gun went off into the floor and, yanking at the arm as hard as he could, he had the man unbalanced; then, by tripping over the knee which he stuck out, the khaki-clad figure seemed to describe a parabola and landed in a heap by the bed.

Surprised and privately delighted by the agility he could still display, Mado leapt on the PITO man and wrested away the gun. By this time a second soldier had entered the room and seizing the short advantage of uncertainty, Andrea made a gallant attempt to repeat what Mado had just done. The second gun misfired like the first, but she was not able to hold on the man's arm, so that suddenly she found herself up against the wall with the gun in her stomach.

'Drop that gun!' Mado called out and, as the second man hesitated, he shot him in the foot, which produced an understandable shriek of pain and the dropping of the gun.

'Grab it!' Mado called to Andrea, and held both men covered until she had the second gun somewhat shakily in her hand and had moved over to Mado.

'I don't think we'd better stay for tea,' Mado murmured and then, pushing Andrea ahead of him out of the room, turned the lock on the two soldiers and set off down the passage.

'They can amuse each other with a nice PITO whipping,' Mado remarked and then added, 'you took that fellow pretty well for an amateur.'

'If I'd had time to think, I couldn't have done anything at all.'

They soon found themselves in the main hall of the joint. One of the hotel girls had a client with whom she was squeezing into the lift. Another couple were just leaving the bar. Both couples froze. Then a number of things seemed to happen at once.

Abdul appeared at the door to the street and behind the couple leaving the bar, Mado caught sight of Graziella-Ephrosini followed by none other than his old friend, Colonel Karai. Mado had no idea if Karai would be carrying a gun but out of the corner of his eye he saw Graziella reaching for hers.

'Don't do that!' he called out sharply to the girl terrorist. She paid no attention but plucked out her gun and fired at Mado, luckily missing although the bullet seemed to go past his ear. Karai dodged to one side and Mado in turn fired at Graziella-Ephrosini winging her in the thigh – not, as he later observed, a difficult target to hit. As the girl dropped her gun and doubled up, Mado said to Karai, 'Come along, Ivan, my turn now.'

The KGB Colonel hesitated, so Mado barked out in Russian, 'Do as I say, or I'll see to you too. Over there . . .' He jerked his head towards the door to the street. It took Karai a second or two to decide to move but then he did as he was told.

'You have the car?' Mado called out to Abdul.

'Waiting, effendi.'

'Then go and open the door.'

'Touristic trip to the Pyradmids?'

'It's a nice idea. Andy, get the girl's gun.'

But Graziella-Ephrosini was a trained professional. She must have realised that she only had a flesh wound and she swiftly recovered her gun, a second before Andrea was on her. At the same time Karai decided to make a run for it.

However, Abdul was between him and the street door, blocking the Russian's exit long enough for Mado – once more astonishing himself – to leap on Karai from behind, wrench him around and plant on his jaw what he afterwards boasted was the hardest left-hander he had ever achieved in his whole rough-and-tumble life. Karai crumpled up, and then Mado turned back to Andrea who was rolling about on the floor locked in Graziella-Ephrosini's meaty arms.

'Abdul – catch!'

Mado tossed over his gun which Abdul by luck, or perhaps because of some early exposure to cricket in British Imperial days, managed to field. Mado then leapt across to the two girls and slipping his arm round Graziella's neck tore her away, nearly breaking her spine in the process.

'You and Abdul get Karai into the car,' Mado called out to Andrea. And then to Graziella, 'what's it to be – a broken neck or are you coming along as well?'

She did not immediately reply, and as he could feel her wriggling, presumably to reach some karate position he might not be able to control, he increased his grip until she gasped out 'No!' followed almost at once by, 'Okay! okay!'

By now Andrea and Abdul had hoisted Karai to his feet and together were hustling him out into the street in a sort of syncopated lope, as if they were giving him the bum's rush from a bar.

'Okay – what?' Mado hissed in her ear.

'Okay, I come,' she said, but as soon as he released his grip, she made another attempt to throw him, which he only just managed to avert. Then, suddenly, the fight seemed to go out of her and she went limp. At the same time other PITO men appeared from up the basement stairs behind the lift. It struck Mado that discretion had now become the better part of whatever passed with him for valour. Letting Graziella-Ephrosini slump to the floor like a wobbly blancmange, he darted through the front door of the Modern Touristic Hotel as the bullets began to fly.

Abdul's taxi stood in front of the hotel with an ashen Karai, eyes closed, lying in the back seat guarded by Andrea. The taxi engine was running but Abdul had remained outside the car, anxiously waiting for Mado to appear and also keeping an eye on the approach of two heavy turnip-headed men from the Soviet Embassy car, in which, presumably, Karai had arrived in and which no doubt he had intended departing. These men and Mado were both converging on Abdul's taxi, but Mado was much the nearer. With masterly timing Abdul slipped into the driver's seat, threw open the door for Mado, rammed the ancient vehicle into gear and set off in a modified Egyptian version of Kojak on a hot chase.

'Where to, effendi?'

'A good question. I think we might give the Pyramids a miss.'

'That embassy car's on our tail,' Andrea said. Mado looked back and confirmed this not altogether unexpected fact. Hm! Mado said to himself and then again, Hm! Abdul's taxi was in no shape for an Egyptian twenty-four-hour Le Mans. The next likely event, therefore, would be an ugly cutting-out operation in a Cairo street.

'Can you make it to the Hilton?'

'The Hilton, effendi?' Abdul shot him an astonished glance.

'I know it sounds crazy,' Mado said, 'but the more public we can keep it for the moment, the safer we'll be.'

Abdul acknowledged this with one of his crooked smiles and nodded. 'The Hilton, effendi.'

The Soviet Embassy car, though still some way astern, began to catch up. Even with the diminution of traffic caused by the revolution, Cairo seemed to Mado to be scarcely the ideal place for a Hollywood car chase, and it further struck him that they were unlikely to make their destination before the Russians had indeed overtaken them and driven them to a halt. Karai still lay inert with his eyes shut, looking distinctly unwell.

Andrea caught Mado's enquiring look and gave him a friendly smile. 'I never knew you were a boxing champ.'

'Worry not,' Mado said, 'neither did I.'

'We go special way, effendi,' Abdul muttered, all eyes, and abruptly turned down a side street where there seemed to be room for only one line of cars.

'I hope you know what you're doing.'

'I have a friend,' Abdul said, and suddenly braked hard alongside another vintage taxi, parked towards the end of the street. The driver of this taxi had been dozing but sat up as if shot, and was then galvanised into further and immediate action by Abdul's terse Arabic voice. Then, as soon as the other taxi's engine started, Abdul drove on and the other taxi careered out unexpectedly like a stray rocket into the stream of traffic – behind Abdul, but right in front of the oncoming embassy car. Equally abruptly, Abdul's friend then stood on his brakes and almost at once there followed the sound of a nasty thump as the embassy car crashed into its back.

'An expensive noise!' Mado observed. 'Well done, Abdul!'

'I think we make the Hilton, effendi,' Abdul replied with a smile.

There was a moment's pause as they went on their way and then Mado turned to Andrea.

'Now lovey, this is what we do . . .' Mado spoke in a low voice, though from the look of Karai, he could just as well have blared it through a megaphone without disturbing anyone's rest. 'You collect our respective keys. I'll get the porter to help us to the lift and then we get Ivan first into my room.'

'But that's crazy,' Andrea said. 'The desk clerk will know, the hall porter will know . . . how long do you think we can hold him there?'

'Yes, yes, yes,' Mado retorted, 'just work it my way till we have him inside the hotel – and the more ostentatiously we do it the better.'

'I don't understand.'

'You will I hope.'

'Well, I certainly hope so, too.'

In the event it turned out to be easier than Mado had expected, although later he admitted freely to grave doubts about the gamble on which it was all to depend. There were not a lot of people around when they arrived at the Hilton. Thanking Abdul and telling him to make himself scarce for a while, Mado and the hall ported supported Karai through the foyer of the hotel and into the lift, where Andrea joined them with the keys.

'Pity some people can't hold their drink,' Mado remarked in a loudish voice, as he held back the lift doors with his foot whilst giving the porter a sizeable tip.

Once in the lift the three of them were alone, Mado and Andrea supporting the semi-conscious Karai. A few moments later they had the Russian laid out on Mado's bed, a process which had been observed critically by a couple of other hotel guests.

'Well,' Andrea said, 'the whole world certainly knows where he is – or they will know in a very short time.'

'Exactly,' Mado said, ripping out the phone. And then, beckoning her, left the room after locking the door behind him.

'We should have five or ten minutes with luck,' Mado murmured, leading her down the corridor at a smart pace. Then when there was no one else around, he went on, 'Now then, which of these rooms do you fancy?'

She shook her head in puzzled misunderstanding.

'Let's try this one,' Mado said, stopping outside a room six or seven away from his own. He knocked on the door.

'*Oui?*' said a woman's voice. '*Qui est là?*'

'*Pardon!*' Mado said. '*Ne vous derangez pas*,' and tried again two doors along. This time he was answered by a firm American male voice.

'Yeah, who is it?'

'Room service, sir.'

'I didn't call. You have the wrong room.'

Deftly using the pass key which had previously got him into Andrea's room, Mado opened the door and, pulling in Andrea after him, entered the room.

'What in hell's going on? Who are you?'

The owner of the voice turned out to be a large angry American about thirty years old and currently in bed beside a deliciously nude blonde girl the size of a sparrow.

'Sorry to break in like this . . .' Mado began.

'You're damn right you'll be sorry – now get the hell out of here.'

'But this is literally a matter of life and death.'

'Oh, yes?'

'Thank God, you're American.'

'Now look here, fellow . . .' Without further ado, the American leapt out of bed stark naked and made to seize hold of Mado, who dodged to one side. The American was obviously well-endowed.

'Hold it,' Mado said, 'we've no time for the thrills. Give me ten seconds and I'll tell you. I mean it.'

The American stopped short, arrested by the urgency in Mado's voice. He was a powerfully built man of Tarzanic proportions, and it amused Mado afterwards to recall the startled look on Andrea's face.

'Okay,' the man said, snatching up a dressing gown from a chair, 'you have ten seconds flat.'

'I take it you're loyal, are you? A loyal American?' This produced an immediate splutter of anger so that Mado at once pressed on. 'Right! I have one of the most dangerous KGB colonels in the Middle East. He's out cold in my room down there,' he jerked his head to the left, 'but it won't stay that way long. Nor will it take his mates any time at all to find out where he is. I want to hide him in here – till I can organise Round Two.'

'Why?'

'Because no one, but no one, is going to work out just where he is – if I can get him here unseen. They'll know he's in the hotel. But they'll expect to find him in my room or in Andy's. This is Andrea Eckersley.'

'Hi! What is this? You MI5 or something?'

'Will you give us a chance?'

The American looked at the Sparrow who had modestly drawn a sheet up round her tiny breasts and was watching fascinated.

'How come you have him at all?'

'George Mado just knocked him out,' Andrea cut in and nodded towards Mado. 'This is George Mado.'

'Hi, George Mado,' the American said, and suddenly grinned. 'Okay, you're on.'

'Look, I apologise,' Mado said, glancing at the Sparrow who rewarded him with a rather uncertain smile, 'I really do.'

'Yeah, well I'm a lucky man,' the American said, as if that explained it all – as indeed it did. 'I'm Yates and this is Lisa. How long do you want to store this guy here?'

'I don't know. Till I get help. I'm having to play it by ear.'

There was a sudden pause. Yates looked at Mado, sizing him up. He had steady blue eyes and a jaw like an outcrop of the cliffs of Dover. 'I can trust you?' he asked, rather like a little boy.

'So help me God!'

'Okay,' Yates said. 'It's your luck I happen to be on leave.'

'Right!' Mado said. 'Give me a hand with the body.'

'Dressed?'

'No, you'll do as you are. Andy, you chat up Lisa.' Then as they moved to the door, 'Hang on, though, give us an all clear on the passage.'

Andrea opened the door and looked up and down. The corridor was deserted and she gave them the go ahead sign. A few seconds later Mado and Yates were in Mado's room. Karai was sitting up on the edge of the bed, a dazed look on his face. Pausing for not more than a second, Mado gave him another quick blow to the jaw and with a groan the Russian subsided once more back on the bed.

'You had to do that?' Yates asked, a wide grin on his face.

'Sorry,' Mado said, 'it's the only tranquilliser I carry. You take that side and I'll take this.'

Without further delay they hoisted Karai between them

and half lolloped, half dragged him out of the room, down the corridor and into Yates's room. Again they were unobserved. By now Lisa was dressed.

'Now what?' Yates asked, beginning to put on his clothes.

'I don't know,' Mado said. 'I need a moment or two to work it out. The important thing is nobody knows that he's here. Andy, go and see if Lars is around. But don't bring him here, not to this room. To my room or yours. No, make it the bar.'

Andrea nodded and quickly slipped out.

'Are you game to play warder for an hour or two?' Mado asked Yates.

'I'll regret it, I know, but okay. How long are you going to be?'

'I don't know,' Mado said. ' "I don't know" seems to be my remark of the day.'

'Well, don't push your luck. There's a time on all this.'

'You can say that again.' Mado went to the door, 'But this is a very big fish, it'll get you a medal.'

'Thanks, Mr Mado, but I have one already.'

'I might have guessed,' Mado said, slipping out of the room, 'but then, you do have Lisa as well.'

Mado was on his second large Scotch when Andrea joined him in the bar.

'He's not in his room.'

'I know, I called him from here.'

'Thanks for the needless trip. What's the next bright idea?'

'I'm working on it now,' Mado made a face into his glass, 'like I once saw George Robey play Falstaff – a little before your time – waiting, patiently waiting, for the next peerless line to drop into his head. You don't remember George Robey?'

'Oh, for heaven's sake!'

'For heaven's sake what?' Lars Sweeney said, suddenly materialising beside them.

'Thank God for small mercies,' Mado said. 'Where the hell have you been?'

'Shopping around. And I could ask the same question of you.'

'Then here's one for your shopping list, Lars. A loss leader in supermarket terms – and he's not going cheap. Colonel Ivan Karai.'

'You have him?'

Mado nodded.

'Here?'

'Well, not in the bar.'

'Do they know he's where he is?'

'I imagine they do by now. Put it this way – they'll work out he's somewhere in the hotel but they won't know in which room.'

'You mean he's not in yours or Andy's?'

'No. A fellow by the name of Yates has him at the moment. A large, large American. But I don't fancy we can keep it that way for long.'

In a few brief sentences they put Sweeney into the picture.

'So what do we do with him now?' Mado asked.

'You think he might defect?'

'Karai? Never. His boss might – as you well know.'

'How about trading him?' Sweeney asked, as if thinking aloud. 'It's a crazy idea. But these aren't exactly normal times. I don't think our people would want to know – well, let's say, not until the deal is done. We can do without Washington in on the act.'

'My people certainly wouldn't,' Mado said. 'The way things are in Whitehall, they'd simply say "Sorry", hand the bugger back and cancel my pension. And I couldn't expect

Marides to make it up.'

'Then it looks like you'll be taking a long vacation, George.'

'That's always been the risk. Perhaps I could come and take care of your boat at Westport, Lars. Something useful like that.'

'If we live that long,' Lars muttered, and told them of his visit to Micheline Bariolet. 'She thinks she knows where the President is being held.'

Both Mado and Andrea froze for a second or two in surprise.

'Come again?'

'That's her ace of trumps, but she's not playing it yet. That's a very clever lady indeed.'

'God!' Mado said. 'How much would I give just to be back in Surbiton trying to keep my wife and the dandelions under control . . .' He thought about Anna and the children for a moment or so, and then abruptly brought himself back to the present. That way lay disaster. Once again he realised he must have been thinking aloud.

'Look, George,' Lars said quietly, 'why not take the next plane out of here? You're getting too old for this kind of action.'

'You should have seen him banging out Karai,' Andrea put in. 'I've had to rethink George Mado.' She patted his hand and blew him a kiss.

'I know, Lars,' Mado said, 'but there's just one small matter wrong in all that. There isn't a next plane out.'

'Micheline could fix it.'

'You're probably right at that.'

'And I can arrange asylum at the US Embassy till you're ready to go.'

'It's a lovely idea,' Mado said with a rather sad little smile. And then abruptly, 'Hell's bells, why are we wasting time talking like this? Let's try General Simonov for size . . .'

'Okay. His place or ours?'

'No problem,' Mado said, looking to the other side of the room, 'the General is with us now.'

All three of them afterwards admitted to a moment of the most utter astonishment, as the local Head of the KGB walked calmly and deliberately across the crowded bar and joined them.

The General was alone.

10

'Well, well, well!' Mado said. 'How jolly nice of you to come slumming! It's whisky, isn't it?'

He made a sign to the barman and then turned to Andrea. 'I don't think you've met General Simonov, have you?'

General Simonov bowed stiffly. 'Ladyship . . .'

Mado smiled but not with his eyes. 'I see you've done your homework as befits a man in your position, *mon général.*' He was determined to keep the initiative if this were possible.

'Thank you, Mr Mado,' the General said with icy politeness.

'Well, now, what's cooking in the Kremlin today? I suppose they *do* cook in the Kremlin, don't they? I'm well aware they do other things like mayhem, intimidation and torture, so I suppose cooking is quite on the cards.'

The General paid no attention to this banter. 'Where is he?' he snapped. 'Where is Colonel Karai?'

He might have been drilling into rock: Mado, as always, brushed the question aside.

'You Russians are always so deadly serious. We used to say the same thing about the Germans – until we had the Second World War, that is. That was the laugh of all time . . .'

'Don't waste my time, Mr Mado, I want to know where he is.'

'I've no doubt you do, General, though God knows why. Fancy bothering about an all-time shit like Karai. However, and I've said this before, it's *you* who are wasting our time.'

Simonov paid no attention to the glass of whisky which was offered him. He remained calm, dignified and frosty.

'You realise that provocation on this scale can only be a matter for our respective governments?'

Mado, Andrea and Sweeney looked at each other and then Sweeney said conversationally, 'I'm afraid none of us knows what you're talking about. George Mado and I, and for that matter Andrea Eckersley, are all here in Cairo in a private capacity.'

'Which you very well know,' Mado added, again pushing the glass of whisky towards the KGB General.

'You have kidnapped Colonel Karai.'

'Oh! come *on*, General! Colonels in the KGB don't allow themselves to be requisitioned, purloined, abducted like common or garden mortals. You know that. How could Karai ever hold up his head again if that got around? Can you imagine what they'd say in the KGB canteen? "Hello, Ivan, I hear those naughty capitalists pulled a fast one on you in Cairo the other day – tch tch tch! Ten years in Gulag to teach you a lesson . . ." I mean, that's not a nice thing to say about your Number Two.'

'I am here to give you a chance,' Simonov said severely, 'a final chance to get you out of an awkward situation. Release Colonel Karai to me here and now – and at once – and no more will be said.'

'Oh yes?' Mado said. 'And by whom?'

'If you're going to play the giddy goat, Mr Mado . . .'

Mado burst out into laughter. 'You really must get some new English teachers on your side of the Curtain. "Giddy goats" have not been played since the fall of Sebastopol in the Crimean War. Giddy goats indeed!' He then added, in Russian, words to the effect that the General should put his giddy goats where the monkey puts his nuts. There was a slight pause. Mado again urged the glass of whisky on the General, who still did not touch it.

'Are you going to do as I ask?' Simonov enquired, as if he were a visiting inspector.

It had by now become apparent to all three of them that the General was not playing from strength or he would not have come along to this hostile environment. But the question in all their minds was why had he come at all?

'If you know where Karai is,' Mado said carefully, 'why don't you just take him back to your nice friendly embassy? Why bother us?'

Simonov turned slowly to Mado and studied him with a frown. 'You realise you will lose your pension, Mr Mado?'

'I dare say you're right,' Mado said, pursing his lips. 'but I've lost it so many times before, I just won't notice it now.'

'How intriguing!' Andrea remarked, unable to keep a scornful tone out of her voice. 'Do you mean to say you have that amount of penetration in the British civil service?'

The General now switched his stare and his frown to Andrea. 'I can promise you that.'

'He can, too,' Mado murmured, 'and that's not the least he can do. One day you should write it up. The public would love to know . . .'

'From what I know of George Mado,' Lars Sweeney put in, trying for a lighter touch, 'his whole life has been one of almost permanent fiscal jeopardy. So I doubt you'll get far with a threat of that kind. On the other side of the fence though, what about you? What happens to you if this present operation of yours falls apart?'

'As in large measure it has,' Mado tacked on provocatively, to be met with a cold stare from Simonov. 'Well, Masri hasn't invited your fleet back into Alexandria, now has he?'

There was a pause. Simonov glowered like a burning ember as he glanced round the room before going on.

'Major Masri is no longer in charge,' he said in the end, 'he was executed two hours ago. Mustapha Khaliq is the new head of the revolution.'

A short profound silence settled on all of them as they thought this one out.

'Khaliq's right-hand girl tried to see me off just now,' Mado remarked apropos of nothing, 'and she used to be such a buxom wench.'

'She will try again,' Simonov said, 'or someone else will.'

'Now there's a cheerful outlook, I must say.'

'Brave words, Mr Mado, will never protect you in Cairo.'

'Paf!' said Mado. 'Or I might even go to a Pshaw!'

'What bugs me, General,' Lars Sweeney said, taking off on a new tack, 'is why a busy man of your calibre is standing here now at the height of a busy day. Something doesn't add up.'

'You are right,' General Simonov said, and to the amazement of all of them suddenly smiled. 'I've decided to . . .' he paused as if searching for the right words, 'to . . . switch my allegiance.'

'Hold on,' Mado said, 'I have to sit down.'

'You are sitting down,' Andrea said.

'In that case,' Lars Sweeney said briskly, 'we must get you to the embassy at the speed of light.'

'Switch allegiance to what?' Mado asked with sudden caution. 'Britannia or Uncle Sam?'

General Simonov was still smiling, but a small cloud of sadness seemed to drift over his eyes. He turned to Sweeney.

'Do not take offence,' he said quietly and with dignity, 'but I would much prefer Old England. That is the country I have always most admired. Alas! I know enough about Paul Tarnham, your own celebrated defector . . .'

'Currently in Egypt,' Mado put in.

'Currently held incommuncado by the Egyptian Navy – to realise that defecting to England might be more dangerous than remaining here *en poste*. Your Whitehall apparat is about as secure as a sieve would be for holding water.'

'And I imagine you have one or two names?' Mado suggested.

'Naturally I have information of some considerable value,' the General agreed with slight pomposity.

'Then why did you come here asking for Colonel Karai to be released?' Andrea enquired. 'Or was that just an excuse to break the ice?'

'Excuse?' the General flared up with a touch of irritation, perhaps at being questioned by a woman. 'I need no excuse. You are talking to a General of the KGB who has *survived* – survived from Stalin to Brezhnev. You don't say excuses to a Russian General.'

'It's a good question, though, wouldn't you agree?' Mado put in quietly, a sly expression on his face.

'Yes, it *is* a good question, Mr Mado. And I will tell you why I would still like Colonel Karai to be released. Karai will never contemplate what I have just done. However, I know something he does not . . .' he held back slightly to heighten the effect, 'we have both been recalled to Moscow. Karai has arranged for me to be put on trial – and I have obliged him, I think you say, with the same facility. Karai will never defect, but equally he will never leave Russia again.'

Then with another broad smile, he picked up the glass of whisky, raised it to each of them in turn and drained it down in one long swallow.

'Now the next problem,' Sweeney said crisply, bringing them all back on stream, 'is to get you safely to the embassy.'

'That is no problem, Mr Sweeney. We shall do it in style. I have my car. No one as yet knows what I have just told you.'

'No doubt,' Mado commented, 'but it won't take long.'

He happened to look across the bar and caught sight of an anxious-looking blonde girl peering around. It was Lisa, the

Sparrow, friend of the giant American Yates in whose keeping he had left Karai.

'Excuse me,' Mado said and walked quickly to where she was standing. 'You were looking for someone, Lisa?'

She seemed almost more seductive dressed than when he had first seen her naked in bed with Yates.

'Yes, you!' she said with something like a whoop of pleasure. 'Am I glad to see you! I was beginning to think like I'd never find you. I'm near-sighted, you see, and I don't have my contacts in.'

She'd be from the south, Mado noted in passing, maybe from Texas. If so she must be the tiniest Texan he had ever seen.

'Something amiss?'

'I'll say there is. Chuck's upset. He thinks he may have killed that Russian.'

'Killed him? How?'

'Well, he started in struggling and yelling. So Chuck hit him again.'

Mado could not help breaking out into a broad grin. 'Oh! dear me, this is no day for Karai.'

He cupped her elbow and began to lead her out of the room. Then suddenly he stopped. 'Hang about. I'd better pass on the news.'

In the event it was just as well they had paused: out of the corner of his eye, Mado saw four or five men armed with submachine guns striding into the bar from the other side.

'Quick! Down!' Mado gritted out and pulled, almost knocked, her to the floor as a burst of fire, aimed at the ceiling presumably as a warning, shattered them all into a new situation. Mado and Lisa lay by the door and as the shouting and hubbub opened up, he grabbed her hand and together they wriggled along the floor and out of the door. Once round the jamb, he jerked her up on her feet.

'We'll do it on foot,' Mado said and pulling her after him

made it at a sharp clip to the main staircase without looking back. A few minutes later they were in Yates's room.

Karai, an ugly colour of putty, lay stretched out on the bed. Yates, understandably to Mado, seemed to be in a high old state. Sweat almost poured off his face and he looked like a schoolboy caught in a naughty act.

'I don't know what in hell's going on,' he muttered, as Mado put his ear to Karai's heart and then straightened up.

'All I gave him was a gentle tap.'

'You did a good job,' Mado said, 'now there's one less bastard to worry about.'

'Hey! that's all very well,' Yates began, 'but I don't even know who this guy really is. And if I've killed him . . .'

'I told you who he is. And he's no loss to the world. Now listen, sport, what we do next is this. We stash him away in my room. That's where the apes will look for him first. It could also get you off the hook.'

Judging correctly that Yates must have entered slight shock and would do as he was told, Mado indicated he should take the legs and, with himself at the other end, they humped Karai down the corridor and back into Mado's room, which had in the meantime been thoroughly turned over, as Mado had half-expected it would be. The lock on the door had been smashed, and his few effects had been strewn about the place as if a hurricane had passed through the room. Well, at least the ruse had worked . . .

'Now back to your room,' Mado said. Extraordinary as it afterwards seemed, there was still no one else around. Once they were back in Yates's room, Lisa began to cry in a sniffy, tiny-Texan way. In Mado's opinion there was no time for that kind of luxury.

'I suppose you don't have a Scotch to hand, do you? I think the little lady needs shoring up. I certainly do.'

Without another word Yates went to his suitcase and extracted a bottle. There were only two glasses in the room, so

Mado slopped out two good measures for Yates and Lisa and then took a long pull from the bottle himself.

'Right!' he said. 'Now for the main news headlines.'

He told Yates of his and Lisa's escape from the bar, as the gunmen arrived.

'The really shattering fact,' he ended up, 'is that there in all that mêlée, with a lot of idiot PITO thugs spraying bullets around, is the most important defector to the West for the last twenty-five years. If something happens to General Simonov now . . . Hell! what's the point of going on like this?'

He broke off and looked at them both with a friendly smile. They struck him as suddenly and needlessly forlorn, sitting on the edge of the bed. Lisa had stopped crying but Yates had his arm round her shoulder as if he were some sort of sentimental Disney bear. Very touching, Mado said to himself, but they must all pull themselves together. No doubt about that.

'Were you ever a US Marine?' Mado asked out of the blue.

'How did you guess?'

'Let's see. One – size. Two – guts. Three – intelligence.'

'Oh come on now, don't put me on!'

'And what are you doing in Cairo – apart from what I already know?'

'I'm in Amexport in Saudi Arabia. Lisa works in the Teheran office. We're both on leave.'

'Well, Mr and Mrs Amexport, do you have any bright ideas? I mean as to what to do next?'

'Get the hell out of here.' Yates smiled as if he had got over something and stood up. 'Okay,' he said, 'let's hope the phone still works.'

'Where does that get us?'

Yates shot him a quick oblique look. 'I have a contact in the CIA.'

'Like who hasn't?'

'Yeah, but . . .'

'You think your contact could mount a rescue operation – here in the Hilton, *now*? I'll tell you what's needed now. It's what the Navy used to do in the good old days – what was called a "cutting out" operation. Like the *Altmark* incident in the war – but it has to be here in the Hilton bar. And before it's too late. You think your man could do that? I'll tell you something, Mr Amexport, *you* may think that. *I* most certainly don't.'

Yates shrugged his shoulders 'He's only the head man in this neck of the woods.'

Mado looked at the American with a new respect, working out the implications of what he had just said.

'Then try him,' Mado said, 'and if you do get through, ask him if he's heard of anyone called George Mado.'

Yates picked up the phone, and to his astonishment it was answered. He asked for a number but was told there were no outside calls.

'Ten dollars says there are – what did you say your name was? Right, for you it's twenty, just as soon as I get the call.'

It worked. Mado's admiration for the big man took a leap. In another few moments Yates was identifying himself by means of some code which, Mado presumed, must mean that Yates was on the ration strength. Then after a tiny delay, Yates said, 'I have a guy here called George Mado. You know him?'

Whatever the man at the other end of the line was saying, a slow smile spread across Yates's face and he passed the phone over to Mado. 'But keep it brief,' he said.

'The briefest word I can say is "Help!" ' Mado said. 'We have both Simonov and Karai – yes, that's right. The first is holed up in the bar with Lars Sweeney under threat from about five terrorists. The latter we think is a candidate for waste disposal. How soon can you get here?'

'You're not ordering a cab,' Yates commented and asked for the phone back – at which moment there was a long, loud rumbling explosion and the whole building shook. The phone abruptly went dead.

'There you go again,' Mado said. 'I think we'd better – well, at any rate, *I'd* better get back to the bar.'

'The word is "we",' Yates replied, 'just get that straight for a start.'

Meanwhile, in the great world of Cairo, news of the execution of Major Masri by the Pan-Islamic Terrorist Organisation had released a wave of chaos which was now spreading far and wide, not only in the capital itself but in the other big cities of Egypt.

All public transport had finally clattered to a standstill. Most shops were now firmly closed, or only open for a few minutes at a time, and gangs of ill-disciplined, irregular troops were beginning to roam the streets, mainly looting, much as their counterparts had been doing for so long in Beirut. It was such a gang that had invaded the Hilton Bar.

On the other hand, some supplies were still getting through, and behind it all, as certain foreign embassies were quick to point up in their intelligence reports, the army and the police were still assumed to be somewhere and somehow cohesively organised, and might be still ultimately in control even if – or perhaps because – they were being kept to their barracks and thus remained largely invisible.

What the media does not see, the public does not worry about. But as to who was in control now that Masri had gone, no one could really be sure. Mustapha Khaliq and the Pan-Islamic Terrorist or Treaty Organisation (depending on who was describing it) certainly laid claim on the radio which they now operated to a general command of the country.

'We are the spearhead of the New Revolution,' Khaliq

declared, 'and, aided by our friends in Libya, Iraq and the Soviet Union, we intend to re-establish a Workers' Republic and to carry on the high ideals of the Nasser Socialist State.'

In furthering this plan, attacks on the property of the rich, and on the great hotels where corrupt capitalists were apt to congregate, had been selectively ordered in token of their eventual liquidation. This was good circus stuff aimed at satisfying the left-wing mob which PITO could bring out on the streets for a specific purpose and which therefore had to be kept sweet. In this, Khaliq was only copying Nasser, Peron or any of the other proletarian dictators whose power derived essentially from a mob.

In Nasser's day, block after block of luxury flats had been turned over to the poor, who had scarcely known what to do with them except tether their goats outside. Squalor invaded the erstwhile homes of the bourgeoisie but once the new owners had achieved possession, they soon tired of the game and reverted as soon as they could to the semi-nomadic existence they had always preferred. That part of the revolution had patently failed. This time, however, Khaliq announced, the PITO revolution would be irreversible.

In one of the great houses thus categorised by Khaliq, Micheline Bariolet sat gazing out at the Nile, as she so often did, whilst trying to assess a situation as it might apply to herself. Now, she told herself, now she could surely rely on the fact that, as Henri had been for so long the PITO paymaster, both he and she had been and still were in a special position. But for how long?

It could be that Henri had been removed from the scene for a sufficient length of time for new rules to apply. Masri had gone and the tail was now wagging the dog – or what was left of the dog. On the long haul she did not imagine the great powers would allow such a situation to continue, but perhaps it was time to be moving on. The clearing-up process might well be as protracted, dangerous and plain disagreeable as it was proving to be in the Lebanon.

Moreover, there were one or two people in and around Khaliq's gang who realised that in many different directions Micheline Bariolet might know too much for her own health. A sleeper must sooner or later be seen to awake.

What she had now to decide was which way the cat would jump, the cookie crumble – or whatever phrase could currently be used to cover whatever was likely to happen next. She rang the bell for her major-domo.

Nobody answered. This was very unusual, so she rang it again. Then, as no one came, she realised with a sudden chill that she must be alone in the house. The servants had gone.

The bomb which wrecked the Hilton did all it was intended to do, but no one ever discovered who did the intending. All that did become clear afterwards was that the gang breaking into the Hilton Bar knew nothing of the brother- or sister-gang which planted the bomb.

In fact, it turned out that the bar terrorists were apolitical in the sense that they were primarily robbers after money. They had already achieved a fair haul when the ceiling came down on them and proceedings ground to a halt. Then, to no one's real surprise, they vanished with such foreign currency and jewels as they had already acquired, and without paying attention to the calls for help of those who had been crushed by collapsing masonry.

As luck would have it, the only casualty of the Sweeney-Simonov-Eckersley trio was the General himself, who had been pinned down underneath a pile of rubble. By the time Mado, Yates and Lisa arrived on the scene, Sweeney and Andrea were tearing at the mess with their hands to try to relieve the pressure on General Simonov.

'Just our luck to hook the biggest fish of all time,' Mado said, as he got down to work, 'and pull him out dead.'

But the General was alive and breathing, although he seemed to have lost consciousness. All the lights in the room had of course gone out and the air was foul with dust. However, with five of them on the job, they managed in about ten minutes to shift the main weight off the General's body and by then the welcome sound of ambulances could be heard. It became apparent that the General had come 'wired', and the recording apparatus he had carried in his left-side pocket had been crushed into his pelvis, which it did not take much medical knowledge to see was broken.

'You might have guessed that he'd even defect done up like a plate of spaghetti,' Mado observed as they tried to decide on what to do next, and at that point they were joined by two large, dark-suited men, instantly identifiable to Mado and Sweeney – and for that matter to Yates – as embassy gorillas masquerading as chauffeurs and security men.

Without paying attention to any of them, the gorillas pushed their way to the prone General and without further ado were about to begin lifting Simonov out of the rubble in which he lay, when Mado with a quick alerting look at Sweeney and Yates said in Russian, 'Leave him where he is. He must not be moved.'

The two gorillas paid no heed to this. One took the legs and the other the head, but at the first move Simonov came back to consciousness with a bellow of pain.

'Right,' Mado said and, nodding at Yates, he struck the gorilla nearest to him hard at the base of the neck. A second or two later Yates obliged the other guard with a similar blow, with the result that that particular interference came smartly to an end.

'Casualties from the outrage steadily mounted,' Mado remarked as if reading the news. 'Well done, Mr Yates. It's nice when the training pays off. Oh, by the way, Lars, this is one of your fellow countrymen by the name of Yates.'

'We know each other,' Sweeney replied with a smile at Yates. 'I thought you were meant to be on leave.'

'That was the idea for yesterday,' Yates said, 'but it seems I made a mistake.'

'He'll have to go to hospital,' Mado said, looking down at the twisted carcase, 'or we may not have him alive.'

'We have medics we call on,' Sweeney said, 'but we must get the patient to a safe place.'

'It still looks like a hospital job.'

One of the gorillas began to stir, so Mado, who was enjoying himself as he had not done for years, awarded him another stunning blow at the base of the neck and then, with a smile at Yates who joined in, proceeded to load on top of the inert body some of the heavy rubble they had just removed from Simonov.

'I like to keep things nice and tidy,' Mado said, and then looked at Sweeney. 'What's the problem now, Lars?'

'I was thinking about Micheline Bariolet,' Lars replied, 'now that Khaliq's taken over the driver's seat, and with her knowledge . . .'

'I think that's something for me,' Andrea said, and began to pick her way out of the mess.

'You may need help,' Lars said, 'see if you can remember this,' and he gave her a telephone number and a name, which she repeated back. Then, as she began to make her way to the outside world, Mado said, 'Hang on, I'll come along for the ride.'

'Chauvinist pig,' Andrea said, but gave him a smile.

11

The hazard factor, which human nature so readily overlooks, had come into play at Alexandria. The moment that Masri's execution became known in the port, and as soon as Mustapha Khaliq and the Pan-Islamic Terrorist Organisation had emerged as front runners in the New Revolution, all ranks in the Egyptian armed forces had perforce to rethink where their loyalties lay. Delay could equate only too easily with death. The necessity for each individual in any position of authority to pick on the winning side before it was all too late became the criterion for personal survival. Meanwhile, confusion grew.

It was in these circumstances that Sheik Karim, or Paul Tarnham, was allowed to escape. Basically, the loyalty of the Egyptian Navy remained unaltered from top to bottom, but there were now local factors to be taken into account. It was generally accepted that had the Russian or American fleets – or, for that matter, the fleet of any other nation – entered the great harbour of Alexandria, the Egyptians would have done their best to blow them out to sea again.

A single ship, however, was a different affair. One ship appeared to pose no threat to the whole fleet, and when a Russian frigate entered the port, the excuse which was proffered – namely, that they had a couple of urgent hospital cases and were only coming to Alexandria for communication purposes – was with misgiving accepted.

Once inside the port, the Russians wasted no time. Whilst

the Captain paid his usual courtesy calls, a well-armed mini-commando dressed in Libyan uniform made its way to New Revolutionary Headquarters and assumed local command. The original plan, which had got out of phase in its early stages, was now being implemented.

The next stage would be to arrest, incarcerate and/or slaughter all officers known to be loyal to the President, this action to be taken as quietly, but also as swiftly, as possible. In this, Kremlin policy, ever mindful of the effective example of Stalin, would not err on the side of restraint or under-kill. A deep ploughed field is easier to cultivate than one where old roots have been left.

Several hundred Egyptian deaths were as nothing when set against the sphere of influence about to fall into Soviet hands. And in Paul Tarnham, at one time the most celebrated defector the world had seen, the Kremlin had picked a ruthless man with a heart of stone. It was small wonder that Karai had understood Tarnham better than had General Simonov, who, despite his age, rank and service, still bore some resemblance to a human being.

The moment he had been freed Tarnham sprang into action. He arranged for an aircraft to fly him immediately to Cairo, pausing only to make one phone call – the telephone system still working miraculously, if intermittently, through it all as it had done in Beirut. However, he did not like what he heard.

As soon as he had identified himself, General Sayyid's angry voice said, 'You are too late.'

'Am I, indeed? Why? You've already disposed of the consignment?'

'No. They are being released.'

'Released? Now? Are you out of your mind? The plan agreed . . .'

'The plan agreed was with Major Masri. We take no orders from terrorists.'

'Ah yes,' Tarnham said, 'I understand. But Khaliq does not give orders. He obeys.'

'Is that so?' General Sayyid said in icy tones. 'Then you had better order him to cease operations.'

'Why?'

'I told you. You have left it too late. You were not there when it mattered.'

'General Simonov and Colonel Karai were empowered to take decisions in my absence.'

'They were not available. Your plan has misfired. The deal is off.'

'Are you not aware,' Tarnham said coldly, 'that a Russian warship is in port?'

'That is why the deal is off.'

'Tonight you will be proclaimed the new Head of State.'

'By whom?'

'The New Revolutionary Committee.'

'The New Revolutionary Committee does not have the power.'

'As to that, we shall see.' Tarnham ended the conversation abruptly and put down the phone. He then gave orders for the speedy liquidation of General Sayyid, and left immediately for Cairo.

In Cairo, Khaliq could now claim to be the undisputed Leader of the Revolution. Like Tarnham, he was an educated, cold and calculating man. In private he had little use for the Russians, and intended to throw them out as soon as he had secured his own power base. For a moment, however, he was prepared to co-operate, the more so since both General Simonov and Colonel Karai appeared to have left the scene, and their underlings, although working strictly to the plan agreed, did not pose the same problems and difficulties which Khaliq had had to endure from their superiors.

Meanwhile, the execution of Major Masri was producing a greater dividend than even the most optimistic reading of the plan had foreseen. Offers of solidarity poured into New Revolutionary Headquarters, some from geniune supporters of PITO but the majority from those who hoped to save themselves and their property from what looked like becoming an Egyptian Khmer Rouge.

On leaving the Hilton, Mado and Andrea had decided that their likeliest way of reaching the Bariolet mansion would be on foot. The bombing had resulted in a scene of chaos such as only Cairo could produce. Everyone with a voice was giving orders to which nobody listened, people were running about in an aimless fashion, some crying, some laughing, and all indulging in a general and pointless bustle.

They had not got far from the hotel when a familiar taxi clattered up beside them, driven by the smiling Abdul.

'Day trip to the Pyramids?' he called out, opening the door.

'Nice timing, Abdul,' Mado said as they got in, 'but I think we'll give both the Pyramids and the Modern Touristic Hotel a miss this time.'

'Hotel closed to visitors,' Abdul said. 'PITO now in full command. Where to, effendi?'

'Palazzo Bariolet, Abdul. We'd like a word with Madame.'

Abdul's face lost its smile. 'Ah . . . that is not a wise decision.'

'Let us into the secret.'

'Madame Bariolet no longer there.'

'How do you know that?'

'All servants suddenly leave. That is a sign. Madame will know what it means. Her house must be on the PITO list. Therefore unwise to be there when action taken.'

'I thought the dashing banker was the PITO money man?'

'*Was*, effendi. Yes, he was. Now, however, that he is in other hands and still in Beirut, where is protection for

Madame and her property? Monsieur Bariolet becomes just another wealthy bourgeois, whose house is on a list.'

'And where will Madame have gone?'

Abdul shrugged his shoulders.

'Normally abroad. But as frontiers are closed, she must disappear here in Egypt. Madame Bariolet knows too much – the way things are now in Cairo.'

He stopped the taxi and turned to look at them.

'But do you know where she would go?' Andrea asked.

'She has many friends.'

'Lucky Micheline!' Mado commented. 'A lady with friends! But all of them at risk, I take it, as she is.'

'May Abdul ask why effendi wishes to see Madame?'

There seemed to be no reason for not coming straight to the point. 'I'll level with you, Abdul,' Mado said, staring at him hard. 'She knows where they are holding the President.'

'The President is dead.'

'You're sure?'

Abdul did not evade Mado's eyes, but he hesitated before answering. 'No. But it is likely. Also . . .' Abdul again paused, as if in doubt as to how to put it or indeed whether to mention it at all. 'I do not think Madame is on the effendi's side – or she may not be.'

'You are, though, Abdul, aren't you?' Mado said quietly, still watching him intently.

'Have I not already proved that, effendi?'

Mado nodded but pressed the point. 'No second thoughts?'

'Word of honour.'

'Right, then, whether Micheline Bariolet is or is not on our side, I need to see her at once.'

'I have an idea,' Abdul said, and started the engine.

By the time Tarnham reached Cairo the catastrophe to General Simonov and Colonel Karai had already affected the

KGB control of the revolution. Indeed, it at once became obvious to Tarnham that the KGB's highly democratic organisation ('democratic', that is, in the Marxist understanding of the word) was reacting much as an ant-heap would to a jet of boiling water.

In such organisations it is very much *not* Buggins's turn next, so that the abrupt removal of the local Head and of his second-in-command did not open the way for their immediate subordinates to step automatically into their shoes. Paralysis might not be the reflex action most acceptable to the Kremlin – to those on the spot it remained without doubt the only safe course.

Thus Tarnham very soon discovered that behind an apparent frenzy of activity, sweet Fanny Adams, as he would once have expressed it, was what had really been taking place. By this time Karai's body had been discovered in Mado's room at the Hilton, and General Simonov had been removed by a heavy squad from the CIA, working, as always, through local talent, to an unknown but safe hideout. This was not the American Embassy, since such a venue would have offered the Russians an immediate opportunity of bringing pressure at government level to secure his release.

At that moment, therefore, General Simonov's decision to defect remained a secret. All that Tarnham and the Russian Embassy could conclude was that the General had chosen to meet Sweeney and Mado at the Hilton for some operational purpose and had been caught there by a terrorist bomb.

Since the two embassy guards who had subsequently tried to rescue the General had also been abducted, paralysis now seemed to sustain itself on a vacuum of fact. The chase was on. Nevertheless, the international situation had to take precedence over the kidnapping of even General Simonov.

Certainly the General must be found and rescued with the shortest delay, and for this Tarnham issued the necessary orders. More important, though, would be to finish off Phase

Two of the operation, which was the liquidation of the President and all like minded members of the previous regime, ensure that the Soviet Fleet was correctly and freely welcomed to Alexandria and to Port Said, and that the New Revolution under Mustapha Khaliq should establish itself at the seat of power on a permanent basis. General Simonov could wait.

Of the many things Rita Morgan had learnt in her passage through life and through her transmogrification into Micheline Bariolet, the first and most important continued to be the simple ability to survive. She had had a more than generous measure both of failure and success. She had been very poor and very rich. She had experienced both disastrous and successful love affairs and marriages. She had overfulfilled many personal five-year plans, and she had also taught herself when necessary to sail into a storm rather than have it overtake her from astern.

In all these activities, most of which she undertook with keen pleasure, as if each experience were a new lover to be indulged, wooed and delighted, there remained one nerve which she kept tuned to concert pitch and that was the one which responded to danger.

Always – even when asleep, as one of her lovers uncharitably declared – she kept herself alert for the stealthy approach of hazard. Luck was a two-way device and, in her opinion, only fools were blind to the extraordinary and fascinating way in which luck picked its own timing.

The moment Micheline realised the servants had gone and that she and the house were at risk, she put into operation a plan she had worked out beforehand for just such a contingency. Collecting together in a bag round her waist the few pieces of jewellery she really cherished, she dressed herself quickly in the voluminous black garments of a peasant woman of the Delta, including a yashmak, took a last nostalgic look at a house for which she had many tender feelings, and slipped out through the servants' door. With a private tingle of pleasure she had become anonymous and alone.

There were a number of safe houses to which she could go. Anticipating these events her choice had depended upon which side would be likely to come out on top. After Pemberton's murder, however, her ideas had changed, and now that Major Masri, too, had gone, a prognosis had become more difficult to make. To go underground for a few days might still be comparatively easy; to do so and retain any power to influence events was a different problem altogether, and after her meeting with Lars Sweeney a determination to save the President, if he were in fact still alive, had grown somewhat alarmingly in her mind and to her private dismay.

It turned out to be just as well she had decided to walk. Road blocks seemed to be springing up everywhere and all cars were being stopped and examined. Indeed, now that Tarnham and Khaliq were for the moment in close harness, the taking-over-the-country process was speeding up to a disturbing extent.

Libyan troops were pouring into Alexandria, and several planeloads of Iraquis had landed at military airfields in the Delta, where the conventional leadership was known to be hesitant or partially committed to the PITO cause.

Normally the urge to heroism in Egyptian everyday thinking can be brought under control, especially where such heroism seems obviously to be pointless. Whilst the bulk of Egyptian armed forces, therefore, may have remained loyal in their hearts to their previous President, the continued absence of leadership allowed frustration, paralysis and a cynical acceptance of the PITO seizure of power to become the dominant political facts of the day.

It took Micheline three hours to reach the sanctuary she had decided upon. This was a house in the El Gamaliya district near the old wall of Cairo, owned by a Jordanian diplomat. There, to her astonishment, she found Mado, Andrea and Sweeney, with Yates, whom she had not met before. As soon as they had brought themselves up to date on all that had happened since they had last seen each other, and had established their current ideas, together with the role played by Abdul in bringing them there, albeit in Micheline's case through a lucky guess, they held a council of war.

'The key question,' Mado said, 'is whether the President is still alive. You say you know where you think he is. So no more beating about the bush, Madame. Tell us all you know.'

'I think he is being held in my house in Alexandria,' she said, 'and he will be alive, that is, so long as General Sayyid himself is alive. Sayyid is the key to it all. He is the only man the President trusted who was also linked to the Masri faction. Now that Masri has gone, however, now that the Russians and PITO are running the revolution, I would say that both Sayyid and the President are in great danger, and that this danger increases every hour.'

'But Sayyid must know that. What could he do?'

'Obviously try to escape. The President is unlikely to know where he is being held, and Sayyid, who has tricked him for the first time, will have taken care to remain completely hidden both from the President and from the outside world. In other words, the President will not know that the coup took place only with Sayyid's agreement and help.'

'Why did it take place at all?'

'The Russians made Sayyid a very attractive deal. He was to take the supreme power – become the President himself – but he agreed to this only if the President would not be harmed, but merely stripped of his power and exiled. After all,' Micheline went on with a contemptuous smile, 'there is enough corruption in Egypt to prove anything you want. No one is untouched. And there are plenty of precedents in recent Middle East history for what Sayyid had in mind.

Sayyid is a man with a heart, but he is also greedy for power. The President is popular enough, but scandal is never more than a step away. By the time Sayyid had finished with him, Watergate would have seemed like a fairy tale – at least to Egyptians.'

'Why are you in the act?' Mado asked, looking at her intently.

'I don't think we'll talk about that.'

'Sayyid was getting divorced, was he not?'

Micheline avoided his eyes but smiled.

'So, not content with four husbands, you were trying for a fifth, were you not? Rita Morgan, First Lady of the land.'

'Don't let's waste any more time,' Micheline said with composure, 'on what might or might not have happened. And in any case, Mr Mado, it is no business of yours.' She turned to Sweeney. 'To what extent can the CIA help?'

'That's stupid,' Sweeney retorted with steely contempt. 'I might as well ask you to what extent you can help the CIA – and that gets us nowhere.'

Sweeney's terse attitude seemed in no way to upset Micheline, who merely laughed. 'Once Tarnham is out and about again – and he will be out now that Masri has gone – neither he nor Khaliq are going to let any grass grow under their feet. They will either appoint Sayyid Head of State in return for what the Russians want for their fleet, or they'll kill him and the President – and that's the more likely.'

There was a pause as they thought this out.

'What would the President be likely to do if he did escape?' Andrea asked.

'Seek help. Obviously, call in his friends. However I don't think he would involve the Americans directly,' Micheline said, 'on that scale the dangers are too great.'

'Even though the Russians are forcing the pace?'

'Simply because the Russians are forcing the pace. Remember it's election year, and Egypt's too big and important for parish politics. Somalia, that's one thing: Egypt is another. I'd lay a bet the hot line has never been hotter since the crisis began.'

'But if Khaliq lets in the Libyans and Iraquis . . .'

'The President might be able to counter with Syria and Saudi Arabia. And that would be that. Only, to do anything at all, the man must be free. He must be seen to be free and he must be able to communicate.'

'So all we have to do is a rescue job?'

Micheline gave a short laugh in which there was no humour at all. 'That's all.'

'Or we could collect Tarnham and Khaliq,' Mado said, a gleam in his eye. 'Since we can't reach Alexandria and snatch the President, if indeed he's still around, we'd better settle for Tarnham and Khaliq. No problem there. We know where to go.'

'Sure, we know where to go,' Sweeney said sourly, 'and we could certainly get in. But could we get out? Who's going to rescue *us*? You know something, George Mado, I think the strain is beginning to tell.'

'It's possible,' Mado said, 'it's been suggested before.'

'Why it is so absurd to try for Khaliq and Tarnham?' Andrea asked. 'Remove those two and the revolution comes to a halt. No hive works without a queen bee.'

'Great as a theory,' Sweeney remarked, 'but how in hell do you put it into practice?'

'I'll get Khaliq for you,' Andrea said.

'How?'

'Together we might get the pair of them,' Micheline put in softly, 'if we work it out the right way. Khaliq will listen to Andrea and Tarnham to me.'

'Dressed like that?' Sweeney said.

'No problem,' Micheline said, 'I have some spare clothes upstairs.'

'I think you look very fetching in black,' Mado said,

' "Keep Death off the Road" . . . but, as you pointed out just now, it's none of my business what Madame Bariolet does or what she wears. Tarnham, however, is very much my business.'

'With help from our host here,' Micheline said, 'who has embassy transport and any diplomatic documentation we need, I am sure we can get a meeting set up.' She turned to Sweeney. 'Could you take it on from there?'

'We can try.'

'Anyone can try. None of us are likely to live very long if you fail.'

Mado had taken a turn up and down the room and now said in a subdued voice, 'When you work it out, we can only do one of two things – lie low here and pray, or take a risk as the ladies seem game to do.'

He glanced at the others in a questioning way. Sweeney and Yates nodded their support and the two women smiled.

'I'll go and talk to our host,' Micheline said, and left the room.

12

In the event, the climax crept up on them almost unobserved – because of developments elsewhere. The following morning in Alexandria, General Sayyid was enticed to a meeting at New Revolutionary Headquarters, where he was shot dead. However, as he had promised Tarnham, the principle bird in the cage had escaped. The President, disguised as one of the fellaheen, had earlier and alone made his way through the Alexandria dockyard to an Egyptian warship, whose Captain he knew to be loyal.

On pretext of shifting to an oiling berth, the warship slipped out of harbour and a couple of hours later hove to on the high seas, but in the lee of one of the great aircraft carriers of the US Sixth Fleet. From this protected position in international waters, the President was able to tell the world that he was alive and safe. The New Revolution and the assistance it was receiving from Libya and Iraq were denounced and, without involving any of the great powers, the President immediately invoked help under a secret treaty from Jordan, Syria and Saudi Arabia.

In a matter of hours airborne troops from these friendly countries were landing in the Cairo, Alexandria and Canal areas. Initially some opposition was offered by PITO controlled Egyptian units, but the bubble had been burst and, although individual units held out for a while, the cleaning up process began.

That evening the President arrived back in Cairo and addressed the nation on television – which came back on the air as if by magic. Bending to the wind from the west, the Russian frigate was quietly recalled from Alexandria, as a gesture of friendship from a peace-loving Kremlin. Mustapha Khaliq at once went underground, as he had done so often before, but Tarnham remained in the shelter of the Russian Embassy, his shadowy role in all that had happened still known only to a handful of people. The operation had failed.

But there would be another day. In the meantime, the question of General Simonov remained to be settled. The US Embassy in Cairo flatly denied all knowledge of his whereabouts or, indeed, of his intended defection. So far as the official and diplomatic world was concerned, the problem of General Simonov did not exist. He had simply disappeared, never having been officially in the country at all.

'That may satisfy protocol,' Mado said, 'but the enslavers won't leave it at that.'

He, Andrea, Micheline and Sweeney were all being driven to the Bariolet mansion which, surprisingly, had not been blown up or vandalised, and to which, Micheline had discovered, the servants had returned as mysteriously as they had left. Yates had peeled off in search of Lisa, determined, he said, to take full advantage of whatever remained of his leave.

'Once they find out where he is,' Sweeney observed, 'Simonov won't live long.'

'And find out they will,' Micheline said. 'Nothing stays secret in Cairo if the reward is enough.'

'And the reward for a General in the KGB . . .' Mado began, and then abruptly stopped as an idea struck him. 'Perhaps we could help Tarnham with that particular worry – and net him in the process as well. Or trade Simonov for Tarnham.'

'Certainly not!' Sweeney jumped in quickly and firmly. 'Enough is enough. Sorry, George, I know you want game and set, but *that* you can't have. General Simonov is far more valuable than Tarnham. Simonov will talk because Simonov wants to talk. He's discovered he has something approximating a conscience – a very, very rare event. But what can you do with an out-of-date British defector? Put him in the Tower? What practical use would Tarnham be, unless he came back of his own free will? And we both know he'll never do that. Thank God none of us can be tortured or forced into saying where the General may happen to be because we simply have no idea. It's out of our hands – and thank God for that as well.'

'I think I know where the General is,' Abdul said quietly, and glanced back at his passengers with a crafty smile.

'And if Abdul knows . . .' Mado murmured, lapsing into silence again.

'Not to worry, effendi,' Abdul went on with a smile, 'Americans richer than Russians. Abdul is working for you. With respect to Madame, secrets *can* be kept in Cairo. Especially when heart agrees with head. Ruskis not popular here.'

They thought about this for a while. Micheline was the first to break the pause.

'Well,' she said, looking away into the Cairo traffic which was already almost back to normal, 'operations may fail, deals may not come off, but communications have to stay open.'

'What's that leading up to?' Mado asked suspiciously.

'Tarnham may very well get in touch with me,' Micheline said, a sultry smile round her lips – the sort of expression which implied a lot more than the words she was speaking, 'and if he doesn't, then I shall certainly contact him.'

'Why?'

'He may help me get Henri released.'

Mado had completely forgotten the existence of Henri Bariolet, or indeed that Micheline had a husband at all, and it was on the tip of his tongue to say so. Instead, he remarked conversationally, 'And what would Tarnham want in return?'

She looked away and shrugged. 'Me, I should think.' And then quickly, 'Oh, not in the way you think, George Mado, with your cheap little mind.' She gave him a piercing look. 'My husband remains a very rich man, a man of influence here in the Middle East.'

'Yes, yes,' Mado said, 'you're making your point. Just remember we work for Marides, another man of some influence here in these parts.'

'What's he likely to do?' Sweeney asked. 'I'm talking about Tarnham. Will he go or stay?'

'He won't hang about,' Mado said, 'he'll go back to Moscow and plan the next plague of trouble. That is, if his own number isn't up.' He gave a short laugh. 'And that's a nice idea...'

'We need a Kremlinologist,' Sweeney remarked, 'if I have that mouthful of a word correct. Some guy who can tell us how the big bosses in Moscow are going to react.'

'I thought you had a computer for that?'

'We do, but I don't see how we programme it here in Abdul's taxi.'

Andrea leant over to Micheline. 'Why don't you and I both go and see him? Or get him to come to us? He might just do it. You're right, Micheline, Tarnham *will* want to keep in touch. And with me as well.'

She felt and relished the keen attention of all three, and rewarded them with a little smile.

'Well,' she went on, 'I might do his profile, might I not? At any rate contacts with the Western press are always valuable at certain levels. I'm sure Khaliq, at least, will be shutting no doors.'

'Perhaps you could get the TUC to invite him to England on an official visit,' Mado said sourly, 'like they did that nice Mr Suslov – a popular guest if ever there was. Perhaps Tarnham could tour the universities, freshening up the recruiting process. Our present lot in Whitehall are quite capable of asking Tarnham back for a lecture tour. How to be a traitor in six easy lessons.'

'There you go,' Sweeney said, a sarcastic edge to his voice, 'blind prejudice again. I don't know why you're so bitter about Tarnham. They all say he's such a real nice guy.'

'Oh! he is. And competent, too. At the last reckoning his defection had resulted in thirty-four known deaths and a hundred and eighty-five imprisonments – my own included. Of course, those are only the people I know about. Your computer would fill you in about the others. I'm not bitter about Tarnham, Lars. I'd just like to wring his bloody neck.'

'Why don't you come along with me?' Andrea said. 'We could hold hands.'

'Are you all crazy?' Sweeney said as they arrived at the Bariolet mansion. 'Haven't you all had enough?'

A large car with CD plates stood outside the Palazzo.

'Maybe we spoke too soon,' Mado muttered as they got out of the taxi. 'Stick around, Abdul, will you? I might still take that trip to the Pyramids.'

'Aywah, effendi,' Abdul replied, but he had his eyes firmly fixed on the embassy car.

As they walked up the steps the front door opened as it had done before.

'Just like old times,' Mado commented, and suddenly found himself face to face with Paul Tarnham, who was about to leave. Behind him in the spacious marble hall stood Henri Bariolet, a little more bent and bowed, perhaps, but otherwise much as he had been when Mado had last seen him in Beirut. Micheline gave a cry of pleasure and fell into her husband's arms with a display of warmth which to Mado seemed nauseating. However, there was no time for analyses of that kind. Tarnham had evidently been on the point of departure and now began to push through the others.

'Don't hurry away,' Mado said in a dangerously polite tone of voice, 'just as we're coming in.'

Tarnham rewarded him with an icy stare.

'We have nothing to say to each other, Mr Mado.'

The guy had presence, there was no doubt about that. After favouring Mado with a look of the utmost disdain, Tarnham continued to walk towards the door.

'Lars!' Mado called out to Sweeney behind him to block the way out, whilst himself moving directly in front of Tarnham, who abruptly stopped.

'You haven't forgotten Prague, have you?' Mado said with a rather nasty smile. He and the Great Defector had last crossed swords in the Alcron Hotel in Prague during Operation Powder Train. That was eight years ago, but Mado could still relish the intense pleasure he had had from the short, violent punch up which had brought the confrontation to an end. Now Tarnham, rigged out as he was in the full Desert Sheik outfit, again reacted with the same cold, contemptuous smile – a smile which played round the mouth whilst the eyes remained platinum hard.

'My dear Mr Mado, your weakness has always been a quick and unnecessary recourse to violence. Please get out of my way.'

'Not this time,' Mado said, 'there are one or two things I'd like to square up.'

'As I told you in Prague, Mr Mado, I don't have to account to you in any way. No way and never.' He shrugged his shoulders. 'If you choose to play St George of Merry England, bully for you – it's nothing to do with me. We're not in the same league, Mr Mado, we never have been and we never shall be. I can understand your feelings. I can even sympathise – but that's as far as I can go.'

From behind Mado, Lars Sweeney got into the act.

'I wonder . . .' he said, closing the front door by leaning his back against it, at the same time warning off the servant who showed signs of trying to interfere, 'George Mado and I were wondering – on the way here – and of course not knowing we were going to meet you like this – if you'd feel like joining General Simonov. A redefection tour, in fact. We could offer you special terms. Accommodation in the Tower of London. A visit to the Law Courts. Maybe a conducted trip to the States. I could even get you on television.'

'Who is this man?' Henri Bariolet asked, freeing himself from Micheline and entering the arena, so to speak. 'Suleiman! Anwar!' he called out to his servants and nodded towards Mado and Sweeney. Mado's answer to this was to produce his gun, or rather the gun he had taken from the PITO terrorists in the Modern Touristic Hotel.

'Back! Both of you – over there!' Mado snapped to the servants who obeyed with unaccustomed alacrity. 'And that goes for you, too, Monsieur Bariolet. Come on, move . . .'

'George! *Really* . . .' Micheline purred in her most seductive tone of voice and began to approach him.

'Stay where you are,' Mado called out, and then, as Micheline paid no attention, fired at the floor to her left, a shot which ricocheted into a window, causing it to shatter with a tinkling crash. This had the desired effect. Everyone froze in mid-motion, and Mado then nodded to the Bariolets and their servants to form a group on one side of the hall, leaving himself and Sweeney, with Andrea slightly behind, facing Tarnham who had drawn himself up haughtily, as if posing for a statue.

'That's better,' Mado remarked, staring at Tarnham in a corrosive way, 'and if you fancy I wouldn't shoot you dead, Paul Tarnham, you make a sorry mistake. You have one big outstanding bill to settle. A death account. Payment for all those who have died as a result of your defection ten years ago. Thirty-four men and women . . .'

'Rubbish!' Tarnham said with contempt.

'To say nothing of the hundreds like myself who have been imprisoned and tortured.'

'You must be raving mad.'

'I could be,' Mado agreed, 'but then I wouldn't be responsible for my actions, would I? And a chance like this isn't likely to happen again. I mean, a bullet through your shrivelled heart would be a nice economical way of putting paid to it all.'

'Easy, George,' Sweeney murmured, 'don't let it run away with you.'

'Very well, Mr Mado,' Tarnham nodded as if humouring a child, 'what is it you want me to do?'

'Come back to England and face the music.'

'Face what music, for God's sake? What am I supposed to have done? Or do you take all your information third- or fourth-hand from the popular press? Let me put you straight on one or two simple facts, Mr Mado. You consider me some accomplice of the devil himself. Why? I have committed no crime – no crime at all. What did I do? I simply left England for Russia, that's all. As I told you in Prague, I've been a lifelong Communist from the time I left school. What is there wrong in that? I'm not exactly alone, you know.'

'You joined the British Foreign Service, that's what was wrong. You swore allegiance to your King and country. How do you square that with being a Communist?'

'You're very naive, Mr Mado. You and Bulldog Drummond. But this is 1976. Read your Marx, Mr Mado, if you want to understand the world as it is today.'

'I have done,' Mado retorted, 'and a right turgid load of old cobblers it is.'

'The world is not as it was when you and I were young, and I suggest you come to terms with that fact. Suppose I did as you suggest. Suppose I did come back to England and "give myself up" in your *Boy's Own Paper* phraseology – what do you imagine would happen?'

'Oh, a peerage at least,' Mado said sarcastically.

'I would get myself a good lawyer, Mr Mado, and that would be that. I took no codes or ciphers with me, no dreary

dreary nuclear secrets – *nothing*, nothing for which I could be indicted at all. I simply turned in the job and left.'

'Thirty-four deaths is a sizeable load on anyone's conscience – and that doesn't include what you've been up to here in Egypt and in Beirut.'

'Rubbish! You talk like some ill-informed half-educated student. All from the heart and nothing from the head. Rubbish, rubbish, rubbish! You are simply wasting my time. The world is the world, Mr Mado, and nothing you can say to me is going to change it one jot or iota.' He glanced over Mado's shoulder and then added, 'Andrea Eckersley will confirm what I say. At least she has her feet on the ground.'

'Okay!' Mado said, dangerously quiet, and slipping the gun back in his pocket with a twisted grin on his face, 'if that's the way you see it . . .'

'It's the only way anyone of intelligence can see it.'

'In that case – as you pointed out a little while back – my only recourse is to quick and unnecessary violence.'

Then, before the Sheik That Never Was had properly taken in that last remark, Mado quickly stepped forward and lashed out at Tarnham, giving him a classic punch to the solar plexus with his right, followed at once by an upper cut to the jaw with his left, which sent Tarnham crashing backwards past a piece of statuary and into a hall mirror. This shattered with a loud report like a spectacular firework bursting all about him as he slumped in a heap to the floor.

'Paul!' Micheline cried, running to help him.

'George!' Sweeney said warningly, but made no attempt to interfere. This would in any case have been difficult, since Mado had followed Tarnham to his temporary resting place and now pulled him up by his coat, held him momentarily poised, and then gave him another stunning blow to the jaw which knocked him out, spinning him slightly sideways so that he tripped over the statuary which toppled down on him as he fell.

'Pig!' Micheline cried out. 'Leave him alone, you Fascist pig!'

'Who? Me?' Mado said in astonishment, nursing his bruised and bleeding fist.

'I guess that's enough,' Sweeney said, and walked over to where Mado was looking down at the great Defector, an expression of the deepest contempt on his face.

'You're right,' Mado said. 'I only hope I've broken his bloody jaw.'

'What is this supposed to settle? I mean where does this geriatric bravado get any of us?'

'It may not get you anywhere: it's done a lot for me.'

'I never knew . . .' Sweeney began.

'I had it in me. Neither did I.'

Mado bound up his damaged hand with his handkerchief as Tarnham staggered unsteadily to his feet and then collapsed back into the rubble. Andrea and Henri Bariolet now joined Micheline in trying to pick Tarnham out of the mess and dust him off.

'And you're right, Lars,' Mado went on, turning away in disgust, 'in the long run nothing is settled at all. It doesn't bring thirty-four British agents back to life; it doesn't make up for the ghastly months I spent in the Lubyanka. It doesn't undo any of the misery and the suffering that bastard brought on us all singlehanded. However it has relieved my feelings. It's a gesture, that's all, one I'm very happy to make. And it's repeatable,' he called as Tarnham staggered his way to the door, 'any time you wish – to make up for all that cricket you've been missing in Moscow.'

'George, something tells me we ought to be on our way,' Sweeney said. And then, as Tarnham tottered out with Henri and Micheline seeing him to his car, 'At the very least you can offer to pay for all that shattered glass.'

'That,' Mado said, stressing the word, 'will be a pleasure and a privilege for Marides to settle.'

'Can you think of one good, valid reason I should keep you on the payroll?' Marides asked. He faced Mado across the big desk in his Sunningdale study.

'I can give you any number you like. You want I should tell you?'

'Don't try and imitate me,' Marides said, 'you won't get out of it that way.'

'Get out of what? Look you here now, Pan,' if Marides could slip into a phoney Greek-American accent when it suited him, Mado could counter with instant Welsh, 'you and I know each other of old.'

'Don't-a beat about the bush. Don't-a try and fool me. No one takes the mickey out of Panayotis Marides.'

'*Me* take the mickey out of you, you old Greek reprobate? I should live so long.'

'Plenty people think you have already done that.'

'Paf! That could go for you, too.'

Mado looked at the Greek multi-millionaire over the rim of his glass. 'I'll tell you why you keep me on the payroll. Firstly – this is my favourite malt whisky I have in my hand. Panayotis Marides doesn't serve that out to someone he doesn't like and respect.'

'That's a nerve you got! Like and respect!'

'Secondly – kudos. Thirdly – influence and money. You may not have made any particular sum of money out of sending Lars and me to the Middle East...'

'*Made* money?' Marides growled. 'You and that Yank are the most expensive double act that ever went on the boards.'

'We'll *join* your Board, though,' Mado said, '*and* we'll earn our keep.'

'How?'

'Let's go back to kudos, influence and money. Who else – other than Mado and Sweeney – that most expensive double act as you've just said – could have hooked for the West the most important KGB defector there has ever been?'

'The West! You say the West. That's great! Where does Marides International come into that? And who pays?'

'You do, Pan. It's *your* pleasure and it's *your* privilege.'

He paused for a moment and was surprised to find a smile on Marides's face.

'I don't say this lightly, Pan, but how else could you be counted in? All you ever do is make money.'

'Thats-a all I do?'

Marides expressed a mock horror, but Mado knew the Greek was enjoying himself. Marides refilled their glasses and waited for Mado to go on.

'At that – I have to admit – you're A1 at Lloyds. Mr Moneymaker of all time. But in the end – what the hell is money? What's money when you've got a gun stuck in your back? Who cares about money in a Soviet prison? What's money when you're dying of cancer? Cash – that's to use and enjoy when you're hale and hearty, up and about.'

'You going to lecture all day? So stay for the night.'

'Okay, Pan, *okay* – so you know about money. You have it and I do not. Where does that get us and what does it give us? I'll tell you – nowhere and nothing. Nothing is what you enjoy in a vacuum – right? And you're not a vacuum man. Lars and I bring you other things. Elissa, too, if it comes to that.'

'Leave my wife out of this,' Marides growled.

'Very well, Pan, but never forget you were able to marry Elissa because of Lars and me, when we fixed Tarnham the first time all those years ago – and don't start to ruffle up. The Mrs Tarnham that was . . . okay, you may say, you might have met and married her anyway – we needn't go into that. The point is Lars and I are two of the people who keep it all going. Certainly you can get on without us. And we without you. Oh yes, don't worry, Lars and I can get on without you.

As a matter of fact, my wife Anna would like it that way. Together, though, we really are one hell of a team. Together – with understanding – we can run any operation Panayotis Marides decides to get into, any operation, that is, with a security factor, and what operation hasn't these days?'

'That's a big statement.'

'I dare say it is. But you know it's true. A team is a team. Look at the residuals we got you in Egypt. Bariolet out and Marides in. Are you with me, Pan?'

'With reluctance,' Pan said, belying the words with a little smile, 'I nod my head.'

'Lars and I may cost you a bob or two. But look what you get in return. And you may achieve your knighthood yet!'

A broad grin spread over the Greek's face. He paused and nodded as if to himself. Then, just when Mado was about to ask what he meant, Marides went on, 'It's in the bag. I've been told it's in the next Birthday Honours, but of course no one is to know until it's announced.'

Now it was Mado's turn to smile. 'Hey! That's a terrific piece of news, Sir Pan. Congratulations! And I really mean it – something you may not expect.'

'And I'll say something to you, George Mado, something *you* may not expect . . .' Marides paused and studied his pug-nosed employee. 'Who knows how these things come about? Better never to ask. However, my old friend, I am doubling the sum paid into your Swiss account from next month, and we are all flying to Athens on Monday. We are going to take a little cruise in the *Myrmidia* round the islands of the Dodecanese. You, Anna and your daughters; I, Elissa and my son. A little family affair. A little holiday in celebration.'

'Cor stone the crows! Or some other such up-to-date remark,' Mado said, 'you take-a way the breath. A short cruise in a millionaire's yacht! Whatever next?'

'And I thought it would be nice if Lars came along as well.

He's bringing his girl friend – as a matter of fact, I think they're engaged. Something old-fashioned like that.'

'Anyone I know?'

'Oh yes, my friend, you know her all right! It's Andrea Eckersley. I tell you, it's all a family affair.'

'Well, well, well,' Mado said. 'Words really do fail me at last . . .' Then he was struck by a sudden thought.

'Hang on, Pan – the Dodecanese . . . just off the Turkish coast, am I right?'

'You gotta pass in geography.'

'Just about the same distance from Alexandria and from Beirut, am I right?'

'Thatsa correct,' Marides said, a twinkle in his eye, 'with perhaps a call on Cyprus on the way – you never know, do you? There might be a little business to do. Now the Syrians have brought peace to the Lebanon, Beirut is opening up all over again.'

'I might have guessed you'd have an ulterior motive,' Mado said. 'I suppose the next thing you'll say is that you're taking over Bariolet's Bank?'

'As a matter of fact, I just have. The old fool is having to realise some of his assets. He's getting divorced.'

Now it was Mado's turn to grin. 'And Micheline?' he asked, 'what's the word on her?'

'She's going to Moscow,' Marides said, 'only on a visitor's visa, of course. I understand Tarnham invited her to stay – although she did suggest that if I happened to be there at the same time, we might have dinner together.'

Mado laughed. 'And will you accept Lady Poltagrue's invitation?'

'I don't think Elissa would like it,' Marides said, and then added suspiciously, 'whatsa this Lady Poltagrue?'

'Hilaire Belloc,' Mado said, 'and it rounds off the chapter, don't you think? "The Devil, having nothing else to do, went off to tempt My Lady Poltagrue. My Lady, tempted by a private whim, to his extreme annoyance, tempted him." I think we can safely leave them to each other, don't you think?'

'Help yourself to another Scotch,' Marides said, 'we have a lot of talking to do.'